Echoes Of The Past

Maya Hartwell (Quest for Justice)
Series Book 1

Gabby Black

ISBN: 979-8-4436-9013-1

Contents

For Kevin – my champion

Foreword

AUTHOR'S NOTE

Prepare to be captivated by the remarkable Maya, the protagonist of this series. Her backstory is as fascinating as her iron will and unyielding determination to uncover the truth, utilizing all the knowledge and skills she's accumulated throughout her life so far. Myself as a lover of suspenseful and thought-provoking entertainment media, particularly courtroom dramas, I've spent years refining my passion, and combining it with my background in the Justice System has led me to this moment. With a compelling narrative that keeps readers on the edge of their seats, the forthcoming books in the series will thrust Maya into increasingly intricate, nerve-racking, and suspenseful predicaments, both within and beyond the courtroom. Immerse yourself in a world that will thrill your senses and challenge your mind.

I warmly invite you to embark on this extraordinary journey alongside Maya and myself. I sincerely appreciate your time spent reading the first book in this new 'Quest for Justice' series. Your interest and support hold immeasurable value, and I genuinely hope you relish the tale. To stay informed about Maya's upcoming endeavors, kindly consider subscribing to my newsletter at **www.gabbyblack.com.**

Dear Reader

I would like to bring to your attention that this book in written in American English, which may differ in certain word choices and spellings from British English and Australian English. Throughout the narrative, you may encounter variations in vocabulary and expressions that are specific to American usage. I hope you find this linguistic distinction enriching, and that it enhances your reading experience. Thank you for joining me on this journey.

Warm Regards
Gabby

Also By

BOOKS BY GABBY BLACK

Maya Hartwell (Quest for Justice) Series consists of;

Echoes of the Past Book One (Published on Amazon)
Room of Echoes Book Two (Published on Amazon)
Echoes of Betrayal Book Three (Published on Amazon)
Book 4 in the Quest for Justice Series Coming Q2 2024 or sooner!

Available in Audio

Echoes of the Past – available in US & UK
https://books2read.com/u/baq9O2
Room of Echoes – available in US & UK
https://books2read.com/u/m0WqvA

Prologue

Eighteen years and nine months earlier

The text from my lover had been short and succinct. He was desperate to meet me in the woods near the old vineyard. It had said to meet at nine p.m., which wasn't too unusual, as our dates often happened after dark. What I found out of place was the meeting spot. The old woods behind the Morgenstern place was secluded, of course, but hardly romantic.

Still, my body thrums with excitement as I make my way to my lover. It had been a while since we'd been able to meet. His wife has been constantly and annoyingly present, making our meetings fewer and farther between. No matter the location of our rendezvous, I long to be in his arms again.

The night is colder than I expected, so I wrap my cardigan around myself, trying to ward off the chill. I, again, wish that my boyfriend had chosen a spot indoors. *Just a little further, though, and all will be explained.*

·····•··•····

I pant heavily; every breath a difficult labor. My heart is pumping blood to every extremity in urgency and I almost feel like it's going to come out of my chest. I have no time to think about the situation but I keep running faster. I can hear someone coming after me in the woods. Their footsteps are growing closer and the realization sends a shot of adrenaline through me.

I can hear the snap and pop of twigs underfoot and branches cracking as I tear through the dark woods on unsteady feet. I feel my chest burning but I press forward, determined to keep up my quickened pace. The panic is surely what has kept me going this long. I can't stop. I can't slow down. Someone is after me. I shout my boyfriend's name with the hope that he will come protect me.

As my mind wanders to this thought, I land on the outside edge of my left foot. A loose stone gives way and I fall to the ground, pressing all of my weight on that ankle. I hear an audible 'pop' and my anxiety spikes. I can't let this slow me down. I have to keep going. I try to get up off the forest floor but the pain in my ankle screams in protest. *This can't be happening.*

I hear the footsteps behind me catching up and my heart hammers with dread. The sound of running abruptly stops a moment later and I glance around frantically, cursing the darkness. I can feel a presence but I am unsure where my pursuer is.

"Why are you doing this?" I cry out to the night, a note of pleading in my tone. The first blow comes and my vision goes white as my head explodes with pain. I reach out a hand in a pitiful attempt to protect myself. "Please."

The pleading seems to have no effect as another blow comes down. And another. And another. I try to make out my attacker but the darkness and the blood in my eyes make it impossible. *Not like this*, I think to myself. *I cannot die alone in these woods.*

Another blow comes down and all goes black.

Chapter 1

Present Day

Alanzi Pharmaceuticals would lose millions and I couldn't be happier.

As I listened to the judge's decision on the lawsuit, I couldn't keep the proud smile off my face. Months of hard work and conviction had led to the best outcome for my clients. The large company had attempted to settle out of court several times but I knew I had the evidence to take this to trial. Moreso, the negative publicity of the trial would further damage the pockets of the fat cats who had cut corners in production, sacrificing customer safety.

Several months ago, a suit had found its way to my firm, Ryan & Richards. The senior associate assigned to the case wanted to settle. I was the one who had convinced him we could win in court. As I read through the case, my compassion for the victims compelled me to take on the fight. I wasn't letting Alanzi wiggle off the hook so easily.

While in production, Alanzi had rushed their new antidepressant, resulting in safety concerns that were swept under the rug. Months later, a dozen patients were suffering from seizures. The company claimed all protocols had been followed but there was a quiet whistle blower who had supplied me with the necessary nudge in the right direction.

I had done a lot of legwork to make this case solid but when I knew I had the smoking gun—the paper trail of a bribe—I knew that we could win this in court. Though my colleagues encouraged me to settle out of court, I wanted the takedown to be public. Alanzi deserved the maximum penalty for damages done to my suffering clients.

There were cries of relief from the gallery as the news sank in for the victims of Alanzi's negligence. They no longer had to worry about the growing medical costs they were facing. In fact, they were set for life. It was a moment that I would have basked in if I was one for basking.

As the proceedings ended and everyone began filing out of the courtroom, I packed up my things in the briefcase my mother had given me when I first started at the firm. A small token, I think, to commemorate a moment we had all anxiously anticipated. Grabbing the handle, I looked around the courtroom—that satisfied smile finally breaking out into its full brilliance.

"That was some great work, Maya. You really surprised us all."

I hurriedly turned to find the senior associate present, Richard Wyatt, holding out his hand. Up until this past week, he hadn't exactly been one of my cheerleaders but as he stood before me, he was practically beaming.

"Thanks, it was a team effort," I obliged as I shook his proffered hand. *Even if it wasn't.* I had done the majority of the legwork and had reveled in the investigation it took to uncover the evidence. This win was mine and I would privately treat it as such. Office politics dictated that it be so.

Richard returned his hand to his pocket, resuming his natural stance—carefully laid back. "Hey, some of us are headed out for drinks around five. You interested in tagging along? It's this pub over on Oak—" He took a second to recall the name. "McNamara's! McNamara's Pub! Best Irish Coffee in San Francisco."

I smiled politely and hefted my briefcase off the table. "I appreciate the invite. Really, I do. But as soon as I get back to the office, I'm sending off some last-minute emails and heading out."

"Heading out?"

I nodded, a lock of blonde hair coming out of my french twist. "Yeah, I've had a vacation planned for a while. Just looking to have a secluded little getaway in a small town down the coast."

It was then that Richard's warm smile dimmed slightly. "Ah, let me guess. A secluded all-inclusive resort. Only the best for the rich girl."

Of course, it was baseless and tactless, but the joke continued.

"Ah, I'm just busting your balls, Hartwell. No need to be so sensitive."

Ah, and a heaping spoonful of misogyny to top it off. I forced a tight laugh and shook my head. "No worries, Wyatt. I know all about your sense of humor." I said that last bit with a little extra bite—just subtle enough to seem innocuous to the passing listener. "Nothing all that glamorous. I'm actually staying at an Airbnb in a small wine country town. Wine tastings, hikes, and I hear they have the best frozen yogurt in the North Bay area."

He nodded, seeming somewhat bemused at my choice of vacation. "Well, you have fun. We'll pour one for you tonight.

That victory was really something!" He waved as he wandered off with the remaining members of the gallery.

Sighing to myself, I tucked the unruly lock of hair back into my twist and moved toward the exit. I weaved past a few people in the doorway and found myself in the large corridor of the courthouse. I had been a lawyer for several years now but the stately atmosphere of the courtroom never ceased to amaze me with its towering columns and masterfully painted murals. It was weird to feel at home in a place so large and drafty, but somehow, it had always just felt right to me. My deeply uncomfortable heels clacked on the marble floor as I made my way to the parking garage, triumphant.

············

Once back at the office, I was welcomed by several associates—congratulated by others. Apparently, the word of my success had spread fast. It felt good, finally showing the others that I stood on more than just my dead father's money. If they only knew the truth behind my inheritance, they probably wouldn't be making comments. Still, that was a story I was unwilling to share, even for extra consideration.

Making my way to my small office, I tossed my briefcase onto my chair. It squeaked in protest and spun half a turn. I'd been begging the office administrator to hook me up with a new chair but so far, it hadn't seemed like it was high on their list of priorities. It wasn't terrible, but I'd often find the chair drifting on its own if I didn't have my feet planted firmly on the ground. The whole office could do with a bit of sprucing up if I was honest with myself.

Still, it was my little slice of the office. I had gotten where I was through grit and hard work and would continue to move up. I was intent on climbing the ladder the old fashioned way, rather than relying on my father's name and connections. No matter what others said, I wanted to know that I'd earned what I had.

"Ah, Maya. I'm glad I caught you." The voice coming from the doorway belonged to Alfred Richards, one of the senior partners of the firm. He stood there with his own briefcase held in his hand, seemingly ready to call it a day. "Word of your success has traveled quickly. I must say, I'm impressed. I didn't think your little 'Nancy Drew' act would work. But you proved us all wrong, it appears."

I would have been offended by his backhanded compliment, but frankly, I saw Nancy Drew to be a decent comparison, if not right on the nose. Nancy Drew was a fine detective, beloved for decades. I knew the other partners secretly laughed at my investigative antics but I'd made quite a name for myself along the coast assisting in investigations.

"It seems that I was able to pull it off, Sir," I agreed, itching to respond to a few emails before leaving for the week. I had a getaway planned and these backhanded well wishes were starting to wear my patience thin. I was ready to be on the road. "Just need to finish up some stuff here and then I'm heading out."

"Yes, the vacation, I remember." Alfred nodded his head like he knew exactly what I meant, but I could tell it was not something he'd been considering. "Tell you what, schedule a meeting on your calendar for the Monday you return. There are some things I think we should discuss."

"Of course." I tried to suppress the excited thrum building in my chest. *Could this be it? Will I finally be made a senior associate?*

"Excellent, excellent. I'll see you then. Have a great vacation, Maya. Make sure you're still sharp when you get back." Alfred chuckled at his own joke and gave me a small wave before heading out.

I watched him leave, biting down on my bottom lip. I had waited years to be recognized and promoted to senior associate. I had started my career a little later than most but I knew I had what it took. I wanted the responsibility (and recognition to make my late father proud) that came with being a senior associate. Moreover, I felt that I deserved it.

Letting out a sigh, I headed back over to my desk and moved my briefcase to the floor. I still had several emails to follow up on before heading out. Work always comes before play. I cracked my knuckles and settled into my chair, ready to take care of all my last-minute business.

·····•·•·····

I finally pulled out of the parking garage around eight o'clock that evening. Most would have spent a night reveling in their success before hitting the road; maybe rest up and face the road refreshed. But I was eager for my vacation to begin. It had been two years since my last one, as I was always so wrapped up in work. All I was wishing for was a quiet and refreshing vacation.

The traffic wasn't as bad as I expected and before long, I was on the highway. Dusk was setting in; the sky had taken on a pink hue as the sun called it a day. The clouds reminded me somewhat of cotton candy and I took it as a portent of good things awaiting me on my vacation. I was still high on my success from earlier in the day and I turned up the radio, looking forward to the drive.

With the road stretched out in front of me, I found myself drifting in my thoughts. It had been a long road to get to this point. The picture of my father taped to my dashboard caused a twinge of... something. Something like love mixed with pain.

The road that had led me to my current situation had been one of family drama, rebellion, death, and reconciliation. It was part of what drove me in my career. What inspired me to be the very best. My father had been a successful lawyer in his heyday and wanted me to follow in his footsteps. I think he'd seen something in me but at the time of teenage rebellion, I saw nothing but a future planned out for me.

I'd made it through my first two years of pre-law before bucking my father's expectations and joining the military after a nasty fight that I hated thinking about. I spent three years with the Marines in their Infantry. Though the work was satisfying, it created a gap between my father and I. He sent letters imploring me to reconsider my choices, making loving promises that all would be forgiven. He was worried about me out there, fighting. But I chose to stay.

I had always been stubborn—it took a car accident to change my direction. The December I was 23, news reached me that my father had died in a head-on collision—the victim of an icy road. Wracked with guilt and grief, I requested leave to be with my mother, who was understandably inconsolable.

The funeral was lovely, attended by all his former partners at his firm, friends, and family. My father had touched a lot of lives and in the welcoming atmosphere of remembering his life, I felt guilt gnawing at me. My father was a good man and in a bout of adolescent defiance, I had shut him out; something I realized was a mistake as the casket was lowered into the ground.

However, my father had turned out not to harbor any ill will. I was stunned at the will reading when I discovered he'd left a sizable amount of money and assets to me, including his extensive wine collection. And a letter. In the letter, he had done the unexpected—forgiven everything. He understood the choices I had made but also wanted the best life for me.

My eyes blurred at the memory of the letter and I blinked the tears away, focusing instead, on the road before me. In the letter he had recalled my pursuit of justice that I'd had since I was just a child: my need to get to the bottom of things. He saw himself in me and wanted me to walk the path he knew would make me happiest.

I realized that I had been rejecting a precious gift. A father's love. As soon as I received an honorable discharge from the military, I finished my degree and headed to law school. When I graduated, I started at a small firm before eventually landing at Ryan & Richards. My father had been right. I loved the work and I loved having the ability to right wrongs.

I gripped the steering wheel, awash in gratitude for the money he'd left for my education and the parting letter that had reconciled our relationship through death. Though I'd never gotten the chance to thank him for his grace, I'm sure he knew—wherever he was. I liked to believe there was something on the other side, even if I wasn't particularly religious.

Turning up Pink Floyd on my car's radio, I sighed and let go of the painful memories, intent on enjoying my long awaited vacation. The song "Comfortably Numb" came on and I let myself sink into the familiar lyrics. I wasn't looking for numbness, but I was looking for peace. Straying from my walk down memory lane, I stayed in the present.

There were still a few hours to go before I reached my destination and the scenery was gorgeous; branches swayed in the breeze of late fall. There were some rain clouds threatening to do their worst overhead and I hoped they'd wait until I reached my Airbnb but such was the gamble of vacationing in the later months in Northern California.

It was late by the time I reached the town of Landsfield Ridge. Its weathered 'Welcome' sign boasted a population of 6,000 and had the poetic tagline "Where the vineyards meet the redwoods." I had to admit, it was a quaint welcome to the small town. I'd chosen it because it was out of the way—close enough to beautiful beaches and the famed Redwood Forest, but far enough away from the hustle and bustle of the city.

Breathing a sigh of relief, I turned onto Main Street; a collection of pizza joints, offices, and a small cinema lined either side. It was a small strip, not really earning the full title of a 'downtown' but it had that small town charm that I'd been searching for. The light posts lining the street were already strung up with Christmas lights in anticipation of the holiday. I smiled at the reminder. It had always been my favorite time of year, even though lately, I'd been too busy to enjoy it.

The town was so small, it took me no more than three minutes to find the Airbnb off Alter Street. It was a small house, with a charming yard, a walnut tree in the front lawn and a smaller tree in the backyard. It was not currently growing fruit but the owner had talked excitedly about the addition of the tree recently.

I slowly pulled my car into the short driveway, and took a moment to just breathe. It hadn't been a terribly long drive but I'd never been a fan of driving much farther than my 30-minute commute. Finally getting my bearings, I climbed out of the car and stretched my legs for a few moments. I had packed lightly so it was easy to grab everything before heading to the front door.

I quickly typed the code 0920 into the lockbox and the box popped open, revealing one of those novelty keys—the 49ers emblem emblazoned on it. I chuckled at the kitschy touch before entering the house and flicking on the lights.

The house was exactly as advertised. Though the furniture was a bit dated, the hardwood floors were gorgeous and the atmosphere was cozy. There was an old recliner facing an inexpensive TV and a large bookcase on the far wall. The couch—though a little worse for wear—was a cute purple shade with a handmade blanket draped over the back. I noticed the coffee table was the oldest piece with the initials LP + JM carved into it. It brought a smile to my face, considering the story behind those initials carved in earnest by a youngster, no doubt.

I breathed a sigh of relief. I'd heard too many Airbnb horror stories not to have any doubts going in. But everything was just perfect. Tossing my suitcase and briefcase onto the couch, I suddenly felt the exhaustion of the full day wash over me. *Perhaps it's time to call it a night.* I gazed at the TV for a moment, knowing that the owners had promised a full cable package but right now, sleep was winning out.

I reminded myself that tomorrow was a new day and I could take the day as it came—letting my whims guide me. This was my vacation, after all. No cases to work, no condescending colleagues. Just a week of relaxation. I fell asleep that night, content and at peace.

Chapter 2

I awoke before sunrise the next morning. I hadn't always been an early riser and honestly, I'd been exhausted from the trip, but my military days had drilled an early schedule into my bones. Sitting in the rocking chair on the small porch, I sipped my coffee and watched the brilliant hues of orange and red light up the sky as the sun rose.

The new day stretched out in front of me and I wasn't entirely sure what I wanted my first vacation day to entail. It was a deliberate choice to leave the first day open. Though I enjoyed my life as a lawyer, it often meant very regimented days. Every day was meticulously planned out—down to the minute. This was meant to be a break from that.

As the sun finally found its place in the sky, I breathed a sigh of contentment. It was quiet here. The neighborhood had yet to wake up and all I could hear were the whispers of rustling leaves and the distant sounds of cars on Main Street. It was a moment of real peace, something that was often hard to find in a big city law office.

I drank it in like I would a glass of Venge Vineyards Cabernet Sauvignon. It had been a long and arduous process, leaving the military and climbing up the ladder at a large law firm.

Always—in the back of my mind—I thought of my father and the gift he had bestowed upon me. I wanted to honor that gift. It often led to a bout of burnout that was only cured by escaping to remote towns like this one. Somewhere no one knew me and I knew no one.

Landsfield Ridge was that town for now. But the next vacation would take me elsewhere—I never wanted to slow down or stay in one place.

·····•··•·····

The main drag was no more impressive in the light of day than it had been the night before. The shops were all expensive and gaudy and the dining options were limited. The movie theater advertised movies that had long since passed their box office prime. The whole town seemed to be forgotten. Not deserted, just existing separately from the rest of the surrounding area.

I strolled aimlessly, taking in my limited surroundings. Though somewhat disconnected, this place had its charm. I had often wondered as a child what growing up in a small town like this would be like, away from the noise of the big city.

This place has to have a decent coffee shop, right? My stomach was turning sour from my cup of black coffee that morning with no food to complement it. Turning a corner next to a large, gaudy sign that read "Papa's Pizza - Pizza by the Slice!" I suddenly found myself in what I believed to be the town plaza.

I say believed, because the would-be plaza lacked any kind of significant presence. Aside from some bizarre artwork littered around a stone stage, there was little there to present itself as a social center. But across from the stage was the promised land, a small coffee shop.

It looked quaint like the rest of the town, but newer than most of the infrastructure. Above the door was a sign that read "Lili's Korner" in a cutesy font with illustrations of a cup of joe and a waffle on either side. It looked... homey and welcoming.

I made my way to the door and entered the cafe, a bell jingled above me as I did so. As I stepped into the warm, welcoming air of the small coffee shop, every head in the place turned. Conversations tapered off as everyone took in my entrance. Some had curious expressions on their faces while others immediately took on a mistrustful frown. Apparently, visitors weren't common.

Trying to take control of the awkward situation, I raised a hand and waved lamely at the small crowd. "Good morning, folks."

Typically, I was fairly good at dropping people's guard. I had created an identity that was palatable and easy to open up to. It was how I found out information quickly, which in my line of work, was invaluable. My reputation had been enhanced with many crime agencies around the west coast. This crowd must have had taller walls than most as the expressions didn't waver on a single face.

I dropped my hand and headed toward the counter, allowing the patrons to continue their gossip. My entrance had obviously caused a bit of a stir.

Standing behind the counter was a woman probably in her late 50s. She carried very little extra weight on her slight frame and the nicotine yellow of her eyes belied her habit. Her golden brown hair was pulled back in a braid and I noticed a smear of flour on her nose. She had a pleasant smile on her face, seemingly eager to greet me—this unknown newcomer in her midst.

I glanced at the menu board before quickly placing my order, impatient to be in a less conspicuous spot. "Hi. A small drip coffee and a strawberry waffle, please."

The woman nodded and punched it in. "Sorry for the look-ie-loos. We don't get many unfamiliar faces here. That'll be nine-fifty," she read off the register.

I took out my wallet and handed over my debit card.

The woman smiled. "I'm so sorry. Where are my manners? I haven't even introduced myself. The name's Lili. This is my place." She looked around the small interior of the cafe, lovingly.

As Lili passed back my debit card, my eyes were drawn to the local newspaper lying on the countertop with the headline "Local Girl Missing." My interest piqued, I pointed at the paper and glanced back up at Lili. "So, what's this all about?"

Lili took a glance at the newspaper and sighed. "Ah, the Morgenstern girl. Disappeared. The whole town is a bit unsettled about it."

"Disappeared as in...?"

"As in, completely vanished. Aleigha has always been a bit flighty, though. Only seventeen and already known for getting into trouble. She'll turn up safe and sound in no time. Any time someone isn't heard from in a few days, the whole town starts jumping to wild conclusions. And then they turn up, safe and sound. Whipped cream?"

"Excuse me?"

Lili gave me a kind smile, her teeth also showing evidence of a long nicotine addiction. "On your waffle, dear. Whipped cream?"

"No thanks," I said, my thoughts still caught up in the news of a missing girl. "And what conclusions are people jumping to?"

Lili gave me a bemused look. "Curious one, aren't you? Oh, people normally start up talk again about a murder that occurred years back. Two thousand and three, I believe. Anyway, they're convinced it was a drifter who did it, but no one was ever convicted so the case remains open and people talk. I'm sure it has nothing to do with poor Aleigha." She gave me a pleasant smile.

With apparently no further thoughts on the disappearance, Lili handed me a table marker and invited me to take a seat in the dining area.

The place was fairly packed, not surprising on a Saturday morning. But I was able to find a table out of the way, near the restrooms. I sat down and placed my table marker down, trying to ignore the whispers that were coming from nearby tables. Whether the whispers were about me or the disappearance, I wasn't sure. Better safe than sorry, though.

I noticed that the table I chose had a newspaper on it, the same local paper I had noticed on the counter a moment ago—*Landsfield Ridge Gazette*. Curious, I took the copy and began scanning the front page. Sure enough, the disappearance of Aleigha Morgenstern was headline news.

There were no leads as of yet. Even the details described in the paper were somewhat vague. No one could agree on exactly when the girl had gone missing. Though, it was her parents who discovered she was not safe and sound in her bed the previous morning. They had not seen her come home that night, having gone to bed long before her curfew. Friends had seen her that evening at a school event but weren't sure where she had gone after it ended.

I sighed as I took in the details. There was a picture of Aleigha accompanying the news of her disappearance. She really was quite beautiful. Dark brown hair, almond eyes, and dark skin. She was giving the camera a flirty smile in the photo, which the caption stated had been provided by her parents.

It was possible that the girl had just run away for some old-fashioned trouble, as Lili predicted. But something niggled at the back of my mind. There was something that seemed off and I couldn't quite place my finger on it. Chewing on my lip, I continued to scan the details, trying to find whatever it was that was bothering me.

"One small drip coffee and a strawberry waffle."

I looked up into the bored expression of a teenage waitress, who seemed to want to be anywhere but here. With a purple stripe in her hair and a septum piercing, she looked like she was in the rebellious phase that met every teenager somewhere, especially those in small towns like this. She didn't seem impressed by a newcomer in her midst or the news of the disappearance. If anything, she seemed to be counting the minutes until her shift ended.

"Hey, do you know Aleigha?" I asked, as the waitress placed my coffee and waffle down on the table. The aroma was, admittedly, heavenly. But I had caught wind of a puzzle. It was in my nature to pursue it.

The waitress wrinkled her nose in a nasty expression. "No offense, but is that really your business?"

Point: Cranky waitress. I nodded, redirecting course. "Of course. Sorry, I'm not that good at small talk. I bet you're just wanting to finish your shift in peace," I glanced at her nametag. "Maggie. Thanks for this. It looks delicious."

Maggie's sour expression softened slightly. "Well, I'd rather be asked about the weather than," she nodded at the newspaper, "that. Just an FYI. You won't be making many friends if that's your opener. Folks are nervous and they don't need someone coming around poking in our business."

"Fair enough," I said, looking down at the waffle. "This looks delicious, by the way."

Maggie smirked. "Wow, you really are bad at small talk," she said, before departing.

I watched her leave, bemused. Typically, I was able to talk myself into any investigation but if I couldn't crack a rebellious teenager, this was a new ballgame. My eyes wandered around the room as I cut into my waffle. I took my first bite and sighed contentedly. Lili really knew what she was doing with those waffles.

········•••····

Knowing from experience that only time would reveal if it was a true missing persons case, I decided to spend the rest of the day experiencing the local hiking trails—taking in the stunning scenery of wine country. There was something about getting away to the middle of nowhere that put things into perspective and I reveled in the experience.

On my way back to the house, I stopped at a local store on the outside of town to pick up some groceries. Aside from some assorted snacks, I had hardly brought anything for the trip. A glaring oversight on my part and one I regretted as I did not want to spend my time shopping.

I made one more stop to pick up some mu shu pork at a Chinese restaurant nearby, as a treat for the night. I wanted to spend the evening in front of the TV, blissfully vegged out. After a long day of stretching my muscles, it felt like it was well deserved.

I returned to my Airbnb around 8:30 p.m., exhausted from the full day of physical activity. Still, it was a pleasurable ex-

haustion as I had greatly enjoyed my hike, blowing away the
cobwebs in my mind and getting back to the elements. It was
something that my father had always instilled in me: A desire
to reconnect with nature when things got a little too heavy.

Settling on the couch with my takeout, I turned on the TV,
intent on spending the evening catching up on my favorite
anime. Instead, my attention was immediately drawn to the
local news that came on. Aleigha was still missing and there
was little news to report. According to the report, she had been
missing for well over three days and I sighed. This looked like it
was turning into a real case. Reluctant to let go of my vacation,
I also felt a pull toward Aleigha's plight and decided I would
look into it. But first, some sleep. I yawned and dragged myself
into the master bedroom to rest up for the day ahead.

·····•·····

I decided to go back to Lili's for breakfast. It was local and the
coffee was good—not to mention those amazing waffles. But
my true purpose was gauging the local reaction to the news
report.

As soon as I entered, I noticed that it was as busy as the day
before—clearly a town favorite. I received the same cursory
looks from the patrons but they didn't feel as damning, or
perhaps that was just optimism. I ordered the same breakfast—much to Lili's delight. Taking my table marker, I made
my way to the same seat. Taking a look around, I was pleased
to see Maggie working again.

The coffee shop seemed to be the hub of social activity.
On the wall, there was a corkboard announcing open mic
nights and cookie-swap parties. Furthermore, there were pic-

tures everywhere celebrating the town. Everything from Little League victories to mayoral elections were framed and put in places of honor along the walls. This town, forgotten though it was, still had so much pride in their accomplishments.

The patrons were clumped together, almost no one sitting alone. There was a sense of community that tugged at my emotions with an intensity I wasn't expecting. I wondered what a missing girl could do to a community as close-knit as this. I wanted to offer my help, but the same community that held the townsfolk together could potentially shut me out.

The next half hour was spent enjoying my breakfast. There was a logical part of my thoughts that said getting involved was unnecessary at best and harmful at its worst. Still, my base instincts couldn't be denied. I was notorious for sticking my nose in these situations—finding the answers.

I was an attorney by trade but my investigative pursuits and the draw of solving crimes was something like a magnet to me; so much that my reputation with some police departments along the coast was held in high esteem. This had also made me a bit of a well-respected detective along the coast. Or at the very least, a consultant. My ability to parse through information and find solid leads had put me in the position to assist with several investigations as they occurred.

Tracing the edge of my phone, I considered the mystery that was before me: missing girl, mistrustful small town folk, a far-fetched theory regarding an old murder case. I couldn't deny it was intriguing.

Having made my decision, I finished off my waffle as quickly as I could. It felt like a crime not to relish every bite but I had leads to track down. I flagged down Maggie, who rolled her eyes before coming over with her order pad.

"Yeah?" She still had that same bored expression.

"Is there a library somewhere nearby?"

She pursed her lips and gave me a look of condescension only a teenager could perfect. "Literally everything is nearby. This town is like two miles long."

Right. "Directions?"

"Head north on Main Street and then turn left. It's the ugly ass building with green windows."

"Noted. Ugly ass building with green windows. Can I get a coffee to go?"

···•··•····

The girl wasn't lying. The Landsfield Ridge Public Library was ugly as sin. With a gauche orange paint job and army green windows, the building looked like it hadn't been updated in decades. The decay and neglect emanated from the small building in overwhelming waves. I pondered if it was a lack of interest or just a lack of infrastructural funding.

Whatever the state of the building, I was hoping that the catalog included backlogs of the *Landsfield Ridge Gazette.* It would give me a feel for the town while shedding some light on the cold case Lili had mentioned.

As I walked up to the front doors, I noticed the carefully cultivated garden that lined the pathway. The flowers were all in bloom despite the cold air—a benefit of living in California. It seemed out of place, this display of care outside a building that seemed so completely forgotten by time.

Walking into the library was like stepping into a time capsule. Despite the affluence of the area, the computers were ancient PCs that looked like they were plucked from a 90s movie. The shelves were well-stocked but few in number. Taking in the scene, I began to worry about the likelihood of finding what I needed here.

"Hi, can I help you with anything?"

I turned to find a man standing behind what I assumed was the circulation desk—unimpressive as it was. He was short, with thinning light brown hair, and a slight frame. Freckles dotted his face and every bit of exposed skin I could see. He was looking at me with a warm, welcoming smile. Something that I had not exactly become accustomed to in this town.

"Uh, yeah. Do you have any back issues of the *Landsfield Ridge Gazette*?"

"Going back decades. What time frame are you looking for?"

Good question. "I don't—I'm not actually sure."

He chuckled softly. "Okay, more specifically, what are you looking for in the back issues? That should help narrow down the scope."

I swallowed, wondering how open I could be with this new stranger. He seemed kind, but I couldn't be sure that his feelings toward me would change, should he know my objective—uncovering the ghosts of this town.

"Well, I actually was looking for mention of an old cold case. A murder which was never solved."

The man's face went through several different expressions before landing on fascination. "Ah, the old Rawley murder. That would be July of two thousand and three. Worst thing to ever happen in Landsfield Ridge. I don't think the town has ever gotten over it."

"You really know your stuff."

He held out his badge that marked him as head librarian. "It kind of comes with the territory. I've had a lot of true crime aficionados come in looking for that periodical. Haven't seen your face around yet, though. I'm Wren."

I held out my hand for a handshake. "Maya. I'm just passing through. I just heard talk about the cold case and got curious." I figured hedging my bets was the best idea.

He took my hand and gave it a surprisingly strong shake. "It's nice to meet you, Maya. So, the back issues are mostly micro-fiche. Are you familiar with how to operate the machine?"

"Much too familiar," I said lightly, glad this was going so well. "I'm an attorney, so research can take me to some interesting places."

"Ah, then I'll just get you set up. The viewing room is this way." He beckoned me to follow him through the empty library. "I hope you find what you're looking for in that old issue."

So do I.

Chapter 3

What a bust.

I sighed as I pushed my chair away from the microfiche viewer. The article was there, just as Wren had said. However, the initial article—as well as the ones that followed—shed very little light on the case.

Emmaline Rawley had been found naked with fatal head injuries, half buried under a fence post July 5, 2003. There were no leads and most people believed it was a drifter who had committed the crime. I had my doubts. A drifter was often the catchall excuse for not looking too closely at your neighbor.

And with a town as small as this one, it was probable the perpetrator was still walking among the townsfolk. Not something that the town would want to spend much time considering.

Still, with no leads and no real connection to the missing girl, I wasn't entirely convinced of the connection. A disappearing girl, while reminding locals of a past tragedy, did not make a definitive connection. I sighed in frustration as I scrolled through more of the newspaper, hoping for something to shake loose.

"Find what you were looking for?"

I jumped a little in my seat. I hadn't heard Wren come up behind me. Turning around, I confessed my defeat. "Well, I found the murder case but I'm not sure if it's what I'm looking for."

Wren scratched at his thinning hair. "Mind if I ask what exactly you were hoping to find?"

For a moment, I considered keeping my cards close to my chest. But something about Wren seemed to emanate acceptance and trustworthiness. It was a gamble, but a highly knowledgeable ally was too good of an asset to pass up.

"Well, I just got curious. The missing girl—someone mentioned a possible connection to the cold case. But I'm not seeing much here to indicate that."

Wren nodded his head solemnly before giving me a wry grin. "That's the thing about small towns. One big thing happens and suddenly everything must be connected to it. I don't know if I buy the connection, either. But if you're just passing through, why such an interest?"

I gave him a look of chagrin and shrugged. "I just have this thing. I can't leave a mystery undisturbed. I used to get in trouble with my parents for 'sleuthing' as a teenager." I braced myself for the inevitable Nancy Drew comment. It didn't help that I had the trademark strawberry blonde hair.

Wren seemed to consider this for a moment. "That's... actually kind of cool. My hobbies are just reading and playing the occasional video game. Amateur sleuth is way better."

I found myself laughing. "Well, I'm an attorney by trade so I'm all about the truth. Wherever it might lead me."

"Hm, well it seems this lead didn't pan out."

"Because a drifter did it?"

Wren snorted. "Of course not. That's just a line the town likes to tout. I just mean I can't see a connection spanning this many decades. Those families don't even run in the same circles."

"An astute observation. You make it sound like you're not part of the town, though." An outside perspective wasn't nearly as helpful but it might mean a more unbiased take.

"Well, I'm not. I mean, not in the ways that matter, at least." There was a tinge of resignation in his words. "I moved here ten years ago, when I was eighteen."

"Ten years seems like a long time."

"Towns like this have long memories. If you didn't go to nursery school with your peers, you're on the outside. Doesn't matter how long you live here, you'll never truly be part of the town."

I frowned. "Wow, that sounds... lonely."

He nodded and looked around the library. "I took solace in reading and ten years later, here I am. It's not so bad, usually. No one is unkind. There's just this feeling of..."

"Otherness?" I offered.

"Yeah, exactly. But anyway, I commend you on your investigative journey but I think it's reached a dead end with this angle."

I leaned in, curious. "So what would your next move be?" I had my own ideas of where to go next but I liked having Wren involved. He was a breath of fresh air.

"Well, I would try to find out who was close to her, what she was up to. She's a teenager so she probably has it all on her social media accounts."

"Fair point. Good thing I brought my laptop with me."

Wren chuckled. "Somebody is going to accuse you of being all work, no play."

I tapped my chin with my forefinger and pretended to ponder that. "Well, they wouldn't be the first."

It was at that moment I noticed a yellow piece of paper posted by the door. I had seen one just like it on the front message board. A search party for Aleigha, taking place at noon. Maybe this lead wasn't such a dead end after all.

"I think I have another angle to pursue. While I'm taking care of that, want to look into Aleigha's socials? I don't know what her privacy settings are but if we can glean anything of importance, it could give us an idea of what her last steps were."

Wren cracked a smile. "No way, are you recruiting me?"

I blushed, realizing I'd gotten a bit ahead of myself. "Sorry, I'm treating you like a paralegal. Would you like to assist?"

He folded his arms and seemed to think about it. "I don't know. There's this new sci-fi novel I've been meaning to read," he grinned. "But I think I can squeeze some time in for sleuthing."

"So, we have our assignments. Meet back here this evening?"

Wren gave me a mock salute. "Sounds like a plan."

Now it was down to whether either one of us could pick at the right loose thread.

···•··•····

The request to join the search party had been answered by the town in droves. I tried counting the mass of people lined up for instructions but the effort was pointless. Half the town had to be there.

When I showed up, I'd immediately been handed a yellow shirt and a whistle. I was told it was how groups were going to be arranged. Each group would be designated to a different section of the surrounding area. The woman who handed me the shirt eyed me somewhat suspiciously, seeing an out-of-towner helping in such a personal matter.

I shrugged off her reaction and stood with the rest of the volunteers. We were all gathered in the town square, which was not quite big enough to accommodate us all, so we were packed shoulder to shoulder. I felt a wave of claustrophobia but shoved it down. Sometimes, sacrifices had to be made.

We were waiting for further instruction from the organizer of the search party—the town's mayor. A man named Fred Westenberg, I had heard someone mention. I was again struck by how small this town was. In a city like San Francisco, you would never see a politician getting directly involved with the disappearance of an average girl. I wondered briefly where the police were, until I spotted a few officers standing near the podium.

The chatter of the crowd began to die down and I looked to the stage to see a man taking his place in front of the microphone. I took in the esteemed mayor. He was in his mid-40s with auburn hair that was beginning to gray at the temples. He had pointed features but they exuded both confidence and warmth. I could see why he had done so well in small town politics.

"It's great to see such a turnout," Frederick said from his post at the mic. "I know we're all concerned about Aleigha's safety. I, myself, have a son around her age. My heart goes out to this young woman's family. We will do whatever we can to see that she is returned to her home, safe and sound."

After concluding his sympathetic speech, Mayor Westenberg began reading off his clipboard, assigning different groups to various areas surrounding the town. As he got to my group, he made the designation to the woods behind Paper Moon Winery. Though I wasn't quite sure of the area in question and silently cursed myself for not looking at a map of the town while at the library.

However, I was saved as I noticed that everyone with yellow shirts was congregating in an area near Lili's Korner. I slipped through the thinning crowd to meet up with my fellow neon volunteers.

I was pleased to see that Lili was among those in my group. Aside from being something of an ally, I had the feeling she was a bit of a gossip. It would be easy enough to get her talking, with the gentlest of prodding. As I neared the group, I noticed a few of them turn and narrow their eyes at me. For a town with an unhealthy distrust of outsiders, they didn't seem fond of my presence at this intimate occasion.

I did my best to relax my posture—something difficult for me due to my military background—and gave a disarming smile. They might be a harder nut to crack but I had made a reputation of uncovering the truth, even from those who'd rather keep it hidden. I just had to rely on my good ole people skills.

I wrapped my cardigan around myself as I walked up to the small group of women. The brisk afternoon was beginning to hint at a chilly night. "Hi everyone, I'm Maya. Maya Hartwell."

There was a beat of silence that had me sweating before Lili broke into a grin. "Oh, it's so good to see you! It's very kind of you to lend a helping hand to the effort. I know this isn't your town so it's quite a lovely gesture."

Most of the group offered up half-hearted greetings. A teenage girl in one corner of the group rolled her eyes and suddenly seemed fascinated with her nails. However, I noticed that her eyes were particularly red. *A secret smoke break, or crying?* I filed it away in my mind as the others began discussing carpooling. The Paper Moon Vineyard was, apparently, across the river.

Lili snagged my arm and whispered, "No worries. You don't have to ride with any of these catty bitches. I'll let you tag along with me."

I muffled a laugh at Lili's frank nature and silently thanked whatever higher power was up there. We made our way to her silver Prius parked on the curb alongside Main Street, right outside of Papa's Pizza. Lili inhaled deeply as she unlocked her car. "I swear, best pizza in the North Bay. You should grab a slice before you leave."

I glanced at the rundown pizza parlor and wondered if it was a hidden gem or just a baseless point of pride for the locals. "I'll have to check it out," I agreed.

As we climbed inside the car, I had to hold in a cough. The interior reeked of tobacco. I guessed this was where she snuck those cigarettes on her break. Hiding an instinctive grimace, I stepped inside and shut the door behind me. As Lili climbed in, I began thinking of questions I could ask her. *What would she be comfortable sharing with this curious stranger*?

Of course, I needn't have worried. Lili needed absolutely no prodding. Clearly an incorrigible gossip, she spilled everything about, well, everything. Only some of it was useful. She barely took a breath for me to ask any of my own questions so what I got was a patchwork quilt of the town.

The Owl's Nest Diner was in danger of closing; Aleigha was well loved, though she ran into trouble often. Nothing too crazy, typical kid stuff. The town's Citrus Parade had been rained out again; something I found unsurprising when she told me it took place in February. Aleigha's parents were quite well respected in the town; Mary's Pizza couldn't rival Papa's in the slightest.

My head spun with the sheer amount of information I was getting all at once. I attempted to filter through it as she went, stowing away what seemed necessary to the investigation. I came away with several interesting nuggets but the rest was discarded. I doubted the disappearance had anything to do with rival pizza joints or a rained out parade.

As we neared the vineyard, Lili pulled alongside the rest of the cars and got out, her boots crunching in the hard packed dirt. As the rest of the volunteers arrived, we huddled in a small circle, collecting ourselves before heading off into the woods surrounding the property. We split off into groups of three, all given flares in case we required assistance from the other volunteers. Or if we found Aleigha. I shuddered at the concept of finding her anything but alive.

Lili attempted to claim me for her team but I subtly shifted toward a different group. I figured I'd gotten as much out of Lili as I could and wanted to work some new angles. I caught sight of the teenager from earlier and positioned myself near her. She looked to be around Aleigha's age. *Perhaps she knew her through more than just the town grapevine. How big could the high school be, anyway? Probably 500 kids tops*. In a school that small, it was impossible not to know someone, if just by reputation.

As the groups split off, I followed the leader of my little squad—a portly woman with close cropped hair. I thought I heard her mention that her name was Beverley. She had every ounce of the assertiveness necessary for the assignment, dividing the group into groups of 3. Once again, I shifted toward the moody teenager.

"Olivia and... sorry, what was your name again?"

Ouch. "Maya." I was careful not to grit my teeth when I said it.

"Great, Mia and Olivia. You can join Reina." I winced at her clear mispronunciation. "The three of you will take the south end, near the pond."

Beverly looked down at the clipboard she was holding and called for the group's attention. "Now, before we all split off," she began, "I want to go over what you should keep an eye out for. According to the notes here, Aleigha was wearing a white t-shirt, with a pink zippered sweatshirt and jeans. It's crucial you avoid touching anything possibly relating to the case. If you find something, blow the whistle and an officer will come over to you. Are we all clear on our assignments? Everyone should meet back here in three hours. Send up a flare if you need assistance or..." She let the implication hang there, not willing to say it aloud.

If you find a body.

·····•·•····

I trudged through the underbrush, frustrated that I'd chosen to wear my regular tennis shoes instead of my hiking boots. The woods were overgrown and uninviting. I had to watch every step so as not to trip on a root. I wondered vaguely what wildlife could be found in these woods.

"So, why exactly are you playing Good Samaritan?"

I looked over to see the teenager—Olivia, the woman had said—looking over at me with curiosity. I was surprised to find that, though there was annoyance, there was very little hostility in her expression.

"Well, I have a knack for finding the truth. I've even assisted the police on several occasions. Helped them find a kidnap victim a few years back."

Olivia looked at me with new respect. "Consider me impressed. Do you think we'll find Aleigha?"

I hesitated. It was always a question I avoided. Missing person cases were often sticky and the outcomes weren't always happy endings. "I hope so. I'll do what I can. Are you a friend of hers?"

"Yeah. I mean, as close of a friend as Aleigha really had."

"What do you mean?"

Olivia shifted around a large tree and stepped over a root. "Well, Aleigha was a social butterfly. She never really belonged to a group. She just sort of flitted between them. I don't know how many people really knew her well."

So Aleigha had walls up? Interesting. It would make the investigation slightly more difficult but if she was keeping secrets from those close to her, it made for an interesting angle. I wondered how much Wren would manage to find on those social media accounts.

"I hope she's okay," Olivia said quietly. Her voice wobbled with the words and suddenly I had an answer to my earlier question. Olivia had been crying.

"Hey, you're doing everything you can. I know it's hard but we gotta stay strong if we're going to find her."

"*If* we find her," she muttered. "Look, I watch Dateline. I know the odds. The trail is already going cold and the police around here are all morons with a badge. They have nothing."

I frowned and scanned the horizon. In a small town like this, it was no surprise that the local law enforcement would be lacking. It was unfortunate for Aleigha. *I should stop by to offer direct assistance to the force where I can.*

I decided to take a risk. "So, there's been talk that Aleigha has gotten into trouble before—"

"Hey, she's still my friend. The adults in this town are ridiculous, gossiping more about Aleigha than the teenagers. She got into the regular kind of trouble—smoking a joint, getting too drunk at a party—" She seemed to abruptly cut off the end of her sentence.

"And?"

The change in her demeanor was almost instantaneous. The girl who had just been openly chatting with me was gone, hiding between a tall tower wall. "And nothing. If you ask me, it's just victim blaming."

I nodded, not wanting to push any further. I knew where the line was and when to stop pressing a witness. If you crossed that line, you would often find yourself with an enemy, rather than an ally.

"Yeah, I get that. I'm not trying to imply anything. Just hoping to get a better picture."

"Well here's your picture. Aleigha was a good person. She made mistakes, same as anybody, but she wouldn't just bail on everyone. Something happened."

I watched my step as I noticed a patch of brambles in my path. "Any idea what that could be?"

Olivia chewed on her lip for a moment and her expression closed up again. "No. Like I said, it was the usual trouble. Nothing that explains," she gestured around at the surrounding area, "*this.*"

I realized the well was tapped dry. I knew that there was something that Olivia was hesitating to tell me but it was being held close to her chest. A running theme in this town. The only one who seemed to want to talk was Lili and her information was questionable at best. I sighed and continued the search.

"Frankly, I think her sister knows some shit," Olivia suddenly said, bitterly.

"Her sister?"

"Yeah, Margery. The eldest Morgenstern daughter. Little Miss Perfect. A bit too squeaky clean, honestly. She always seemed shifty to me. She works at Lili's on weekends sometimes. You might be able to catch her there."

I didn't point out the dichotomy of her sentence and nodded instead. "I'll speak with her if I have the chance."

"Girls." Reina finally spoke. "We really need to be focused more on *searching*."

"Right, Mrs. Arthur. I'm sorry." Olivia moved past me and headed deeper into the woods, calling out Aleigha's name.

I stood there for a moment, absorbing everything that I had just been told. In all of Lili's chatter, she'd never mentioned a sister. In fact, I'd yet to hear her mentioned by the townsfolk at all. It seemed like a conversation was in order.

"Hey! Over here, I think I found something!"

A whistle blew then and I ran toward the commotion. As I approached, I saw Reina and one of the officers hunched over a fallen branch, eyeing a piece of blue cloth suspiciously. Upon further investigation, I realized it was only a property marker, information I had picked up when searching for a missing boy the year prior, and we pressed on.

Chapter 4

The search party—as I'd anticipated—had yielded nothing. In my experience, search parties were a way for the townspeople to feel like they were contributing. It rarely ever came of anything, though. The crew of volunteers gathered at dusk in the plaza and dispersed in a haze of disappointment. I understood the need to feel like you were doing something and I felt for them.

As soon as I arrived back at the square, I headed for the library, hoping that Wren had better luck with his end of the investigation. No dice. He had scoured all of her socials—Instagram, TikTok, Twitter, apparently no Facebook—and had found a whole lot of nothing. There were pictures of her in large groups at parties and school events. Some pictures of her cheering at homecoming, complaints about difficult geometry tests, just regular teen stuff. No evidence of anything nefarious.

I thanked Wren for his work and headed back to the Airbnb, ready to crash. As I clicked on the lights and looked around the quaint little living room, I wondered about the person who lived here when it wasn't being rented. I had begun looking at everyone in town as potential suspects and suddenly, even this innocent little parsonage seemed like it could be hiding dark secrets.

My stomach made a truly wretched noise and I realized that I hadn't eaten since breakfast. I sighed and made my way to the couch. Plopping down, I pulled out my phone and began scrolling through takeout options. There weren't many but I eventually settled on a small veggie pizza from Papa's. I figured with Lili's endorsement, it was a viable option.

When the pizza arrived, I was too exhausted to go hunting for dinnerware. Instead, I ate it straight from the box while I binge watched a new anime on CrunchyRoll. It was a guilty pleasure of mine, something that I did not advertise to many acquaintances—especially my colleagues. It was hard enough to be taken seriously without admitting to being a dork in my spare time.

Still, I was unable to keep my mind from wandering to the case at hand. The subtitles slipped by as I considered Aleigha and what Olivia didn't want to tell me. Was it something signif-icant enough to have gotten her into trouble? Or was it just a friend being protected from nasty rumors?

After just one episode that I had barely watched, I clicked off the TV and sighed. My stomach gurgled ominously and I had my doubts about the supremacy of Papa's Pizza. Or maybe the case was getting to me; I could feel a headache coming on as well. Stowing away the remainder of the pizza in the fridge, I began getting ready for bed. Slipping into the cotton pajamas that my mother had gotten me last Christmas, I went into the bathroom to wash my face and brush my teeth. The ritual of it settled my anxious nerves. *You're supposed to be relaxing this week. Not chasing a ghost.*

A case had found me, though. And I had to follow it to its conclusion. It was a leftover from my sleuthing days. Not that those had ever really ended. I was incurably curious and could never leave well enough alone.

Shutting off the tap, I entered the bedroom and climbed into bed. Tomorrow would be a new day, which would hopefully mean new leads. I decided I'd try to track down Margery. It was possible she had insights and the willingness to share them. These were my last thoughts as I drifted into sleep, enveloped by the absurdly comfortable bed.

·····•••·····

I slept in a little later than I had intended. Wasting no time, I slipped on a simple outfit: a red knit sweater, jeans, and a pair of sneakers that I had packed as backup. The ones from the day before had gotten trashed out in the woods. Ignoring the coffee maker on the kitchen island, I grabbed my keys and headed into town to Lili's Korner.

The place was just as busy on a Monday, something I found surprising. I made my way to the counter to a smiling Lili.

"Another strawberry waffle, Maya?"

I scanned the dining area and saw a different teenage girl running orders to the scattered tables. *Margery, maybe?*

"Uh, I think I'll actually go with a danish today. And a large drip coffee."

"Ooh, shaking things up a little. I like it." Lili did a little wiggle in place that managed to bring a smile to my face. A hopeless gossip, she was. But she was also a fairly lovable person.

After paying for my meal, I took my order marker to a table in the young woman's section, seating myself near the window. There was another newspaper on the table. The *Landsfield Ridge Gazette* had front page coverage of the search efforts; a picture of the mayor with a group of volunteers was plastered above the piece.

They managed to put a positive spin on it somehow, turning it into a piece that was mostly fluff. Buzz phrases like "strength of community" and "small town pride" were littered throughout. It turned my stomach so I flipped it over. Nothing of importance there.

"Large coffee and a cherry danish?"

I looked up from the abandoned paper and realized the new waitress was standing over me with my order. Her expression was one of stone.

"That would be me," I peeked at her name tag, "Margery."

Margery's eyes widened for a second before they darted down to her name tag. "Uh, yeah. Well, here's your breakfast. Will you be needing anything else?"

I took a cursory look over my order and shook my head. "No. But, uh, are you going on break soon?"

Her eyes suddenly narrowed. "Um. Why?"

I patted the seat beside me. "I'm an investigator. I just wanted to ask you a few questions about your sister. Just hoping to be of help."

Margery clenched her teeth and looked around the room, as if for rescue. "Look, I don't really know if I want to take my break to talk to some stranger..."

"It won't take long at all. I just figured you would know her best. I want to help find her if I can."

After a moment, Margery motioned to Lili and plopped down in the seat across from me. "I don't exactly know how much help I can be."

"Why do you say that?" I found it was often helpful to let the other person guide the conversation. It made them more willing to open up.

She fidgeted with a lock of hair and glanced everywhere but at me. "Well, you know how it is with sisters. We make it a point not to know each other too well. Plus, she's two years younger than me. We don't even socialize in the same circles."

"I was told that Aleigha socializes in a lot of circles."

There was a moment where a passing emotion flickered across Margery's face but before I could identify it, she was back to her smooth mask. "Yes, she's definitely popular. I mean, how could she not be?"

I noticed for the first time the contrast between Margery and the girl in the newspaper. Where Aleigha was all beauty and poise, Margery was slightly plump with her hair cut in a style that didn't suit her features. Her glasses were outdated and she had the telltale signs of acne beneath her makeup.

Suddenly the twinge of annoyance in her voice made sense. *A sibling rivalry. I shouldn't be surprised.* I had run into them in more cases than I could count. It was an age-old tradition. Still, there was something else there. Something beyond jealousy. As she shifted in her seat, I realized that there were cards she was playing close to her chest.

"And you can't think of any reason your sister might take off? Or be the victim of foul play?"

At that, Margery jumped out of her seat, her face turning three different shades of red in seconds. "Get out!"

You could have heard a pin drop in the cafe. Every patron turned to stare at the scene unfolding. Even the employees slowed their steps to rubberneck.

"I'm sorry, I didn't mean to upset you." I fished in my wallet for a tip and my card. I placed them both down on the table. "I know this must be hard but I really am just trying to help. If you think of anything..." I tapped the card.

Margery said nothing. Not a single word. It was more troubling than the yelling. Her face was a twisted mask of utter rage
and her fists shook at her sides. I looked around at the patrons
and staff in the cafe with an apologetic nod before departing.
My cheeks burned as I briskly walked through the front door,
dozens of eyes pointed at me. As I stepped into the square, I
continued my clipped pace toward my car.

Not your greatest moment, Hartwell.

I still had one more place to try, though. Hopefully this one
went a little better.

··········

"Absolutely not. You can't be serious!"

I was standing in the office of the chief of the Landsfield
Ridge police force—Robbie Strong. He was leaning forward in
his chair giving me an icy glare that almost felt like it could give
me frostbite. I had just offered to assist with the investigation,
citing my experience with other departments. And he was responding like I'd asked if I could sacrifice a goat on his desk.

"Look, I know it's a bit unorthodox. But I have been a valuable asset in several other investigations along the coast. I'm
well known at my local precinct—"

"Where's your badge, Miss Hartwell?"

It took everything in me not to sigh. "As I stated before, I'm
not a cop. I'm an attorney."

Chief Strong leaned back in his chair and shook his head.
"Look, Miss Hartwell. Maybe in San Francisco they let anyone
play cop but I'm not about to let some amateur snoop trample
my investigation to get their kicks."

Bristling, I fought to keep my voice steady. "I am a highly trained veteran with several solved cases under my belt. I am no amateur, nor am I going to trample anyone's investigation. I'm merely asking to assist."

"Is that what you were doing with Margery Morgenstern an hour ago?"

I swallowed. I hadn't been expecting that. "What?"

"Yeah, a little bit before you arrived, I got a phone call from Lili Ellis. It seems you caused quite a ruckus in her establishment. Upset Miss Morgenstern quite badly. Poor thing was sobbing. Is that your idea of being highly trained and capable?"

"I merely asked—"

"You played cop. Leave the investigation to the professionals. Furthermore, don't be harassing that poor family. If they want your help, they'll ask for it. Otherwise, you stay away from them, ya hear?"

I suddenly felt like I was back in grade school, being scolded by the principal. I had gone about this all wrong. Excited to be back in the field, I had stepped on a few toes. I made a mental note to always check with law enforcement before I began investigating.

"You're right. I will leave the investigation to the... professionals." I left a beat before professionals, adding just a touch of derision to my tone. Not enough to be called out but enough to get under his skin.

I knew how things often worked in small departments like this. The most excitement they saw was busting kids for smoking pot under the bleachers. They were in over their heads with anything more serious. It was why the cold case in the early 2000s had gone unsolved. It's why they were probably chasing their tails in this investigation. Still, there was not much else I could do. It was a slammed door.

I collected my things slowly and made my way to the door. "Should *you* change your mind..." I placed my card on his desk.

I could've sworn I saw a vein pulse out of his forehead with the force of a geyser. After a moment, he sighed. "Look, I'm sure you know quite well that this town doesn't take kindly to new arrivals. You have to understand," he paused, "a nobody showing up on 'vacation' and aggravating the residents doesn't look good."

"I have a real knack for this kind of thing."

"Miss Hartwell, please take comfort in knowing we are doing all we can. Thank you for your assistance in the search party, that was mighty kind of you, considering you don't have any ties to this town. If you really want to help, let me do my job and stay out of it!"

I decided not to press my luck any further. Strolling through the bullpen, I was wholly aware of the attention I was receiving. This was just a day for making waves, it seemed. I wasn't going to allow that to deter me. You didn't become a high-powered female attorney by avoiding rocking the boat. Still, it could put a hitch in my investigative pursuits.

As I exited the police station, stepping once again into the bright day, I looked up and down the street, trying to assess my next move. With no other ideas, I decided a visit with Wren was probably due. Perhaps he had uncovered something in the time that I had been away. Also, I craved the company of someone who was on my side.

Lifting my head up and squaring my shoulders, I walked in the direction of the library. As I walked through the town, I began to see it in a different light. What once seemed quaint and lost in time now seemed secretive and closed off. The townspeople had all shared a distrust of my presence, aside from Wren. Lili had been an ally too, I reminded myself. But that was probably out the window after I had made her employee cry in the middle of a shift.

As I neared the library, I began to wonder if this investigation was even worth it. No one seemed to want me looking into this. For the most part, they had been the opposite of helpful. However, those tiny glimpses of secrets kept and words unspoken left me wanting to continue down this path.

I welcomed the warmth of the library as I stepped inside. Wren wasn't at the circulation desk, though. I quickly scanned the room for him but wasn't able to see him among the stacks. It didn't seem like anyone was there. *Odd.*

"Oh, hello."

I jumped, startled at the unexpected voice. Wren stood up from where he'd been kneeling on the floor beside a shelf. "Sorry, I didn't see you come in. What do you need?"

"Honestly? A stiff drink."

Wren put down a handful of paperbacks and gave me a sympathetic smile. "Still no luck on your front?"

I blew out a frustrated sigh and ran my fingers through my hair, leaning against the desk. "Well, that's the thing. I keep getting hints of leads. But the second I hone in on anything, people start clamming up."

"Welcome to Landsfield Ridge. We're experts at dancing around a topic."

"I'm beginning to get that." I chewed on my bottom lip. "I thought my reputation with law enforcement would get me somewhere with the department here but—"

"They got macho about it and spit on your credentials. Once again, welcome to Landsfield Ridge. Where every cop was a bully in high school."

I tapped my fingers against the desk, thinking through my remaining options. "Well, there seems to be something about

Aleigha that none of the teenagers want to tell me. Any idea what that could be?"

Wren held up his hands in a helpless expression. "Sorry, I'm not really up on my teenage girl gossip. But I can comb back over her social media accounts. Maybe check out some of her friends' pages. They might give us information that her account didn't."

That actually wasn't a terrible idea. I cursed myself for not having thought of it. Despite it coming up in several cases, I'd always been resistant to social media. Which meant that I didn't quite grasp its utilization. It was a glaring chink in my armor.

"Sure, we can get started on that—" My sentence was cut off by the ring of my cell phone. I glanced at it, considering letting it go to voicemail. It was undoubtedly an impatient colleague or a paralegal who couldn't figure something out. I was on vacation, of course, but that didn't mean the work ever really ended.

I pulled out the phone, intent on hitting ignore, when I saw the number on the screen. It was unfamiliar but the area code matched this town. *Had the chief changed his mind?* If he had, that was the quickest change of heart I had ever witnessed. I answered before it went to voicemail.

"This is Maya Hartwell."

Wren lifted an eyebrow in my direction and wryly pointed at the "No Cellphones Allowed" sign. Giving him an apologetic expression, I headed for the front door. But the voice on the other line stopped me in my tracks.

"Yes, I believe you gave this card to my daughter? This is Evelyn Morgenstern. If you're still willing to help, we're willing to speak with you. We could use every resource at our disposal and we've heard of you. The Patterson case in Petaluma not long ago."

·····•··•····

I filled Wren in following the conversation. Leaving him to look into the social media accounts on his own, I headed to the Morgenstern household to speak to Aleigha's parents. Apparently, when they heard about the incident in the coffee shop, they weren't as quick to discount my offer as their daughter had been. When she turned the card over to them, they'd decided to give me a call.

Their house was past the river, out toward where Paper Moon Winery had been. I followed my GPS to the destination faithfully, only to find that the house sat squarely on the same property. Apparently, the Morgenstern family were doing okay for themselves. I climbed out of the car and walked up the short driveway to the front door. Before I had a chance to knock, it flew open and a thin, middle-aged woman who looked sick with worry stood in the entrance.

"Miss Hartwell?"

I gave her a reassuring smile and stuck my hands in the pockets of my jeans. "Just Maya is fine. You wanted to talk?"

She looked surprised, even though she was the one who had invited me. "Oh yes! Of course, of course. Come on in. Matthew is in the study. I'll go fetch him. You can make yourself at home in the parlor."

I dutifully took a seat and looked around. It was an old house, but well-looked after. The hardwood floors were gorgeous and every piece of furniture seemed to be in pristine condition.

In fact, everything I could see was absolutely immaculate. I couldn't believe that two teenagers lived under this roof.

My observations were interrupted by Evelyn entering the room, her husband in tow. "Can I get you anything? Coffee? Tea?"

I waved off her concern with a small smile. "I'm fine, really."

Matthew took the lead from there. "First of all, we want to apologize for our daughter's behavior. She has always been a bit—theatrical. She had no right to treat you like that."

"I upset her, it's understandable."

Matthew frowned and shook his head vehemently. "It is never understandable to treat an elder in such a way."

Ah, old school parenting. "Well, either way, I harbor no ill will. I just want to do what I can to help you find your daughter. Can you tell me about her?"

Tears immediately began to flow down Evelyn's face. "She is a lovely girl. Just—just the sweetest, darling girl."

This was typical in parent interviews but it did little for my investigation. I hoped that Matthew would be able to give me a more clear picture of his daughter and anything she might be involved with.

"She was just—our miracle child," Evelyn sniffled.

That piqued my interest. "Your miracle child?"

Evelyn merely nodded and continued to cry into a kleenex. Matthew rested a reassuring hand on her leg and turned to me, taking the reins from his wife. "After Margery, Evelyn was told she could never get pregnant again. We thought we wouldn't have any more children. But then Aleigha came into our lives."

"Sorry, came into your lives?"

"She's adopted. See, my wife's family owns this vineyard. But I'm actually a surgeon. I commute to Santa Rosa every day to Memorial Hospital. Aleigha came to us after a relief mission to Israel. Poor thing had gotten caught in a blast. The other doctors didn't think they'd be able to save her leg." His voice wavered at the memory.

"Her parents died in the blast. So she was all alone," Evelyn said, having regained her composure. "Matthew took great care of her and I began visiting her and eventually, we were able to adopt. It took years and a decent legal battle but we were granted the adoption right as she turned four."

"That's beautiful," I said. And I honestly meant it.

Evelyn wiped away a few stray tears. "Anyway, she's been our little miracle ever since."

I looked at the mantel and noticed that they definitely cared quite a lot about their adopted daughter. There were numerous pictures of her cheering at games, an eighth grade graduation photo; even one of her riding a horse. In fact, I noticed that her pictures far outnumbered the ones that depicted Margery. *Maybe the sibling rivalry angle isn't so far off.* "Can you think of anything that might help the investigation? Does Aleigha have a boyfriend? Did she seem a little off in the days leading up to her disappearance?"

The couple looked at each other briefly as they both searched their memories.

"No boyfriends that we know of. She likes to go on dates, nothing serious, though," Matthew finally said. "And as for acting strange, I thought it was nothing at the time but she had started double checking the locks. I asked her about it but she always shrugged it off with a joke. That was always her style." He smiled, his eyes getting misty. "Didn't want to worry her old man."

So Aleigha had some idea of the danger.

We talked for the next 20 minutes but I got nothing else aside from the usual runaround. The problem with discussing these matters with parents is that they were unlikely to see past their rose colored glasses. To them, their kid was perfect and it was often difficult to pry loose anything useful. Still, I had some solid leads from the conversation. *Maybe Wren had had some luck as well.*

As I made my way to my car, I called him, having exchanged numbers before I left the library—something he was much too excited about. I listened to the dial tone as I got in the car.

"Maya?" Wren's voice finally answered.

"The one and only."

"Are you sitting down? Because I think I just made a break-through."

I climbed into my car and slammed the door behind me. I stuck my key in the ignition but waited for a response before turning it. "Well? Are you going to make me guess?"

He huffed on the line. "Fine, ruin the buildup. I found a second Instagram account. Aleigha has two profiles."

Chapter 5

It was after hours by the time I arrived at the public library, but I knew Wren was still inside, awaiting my arrival. I tapped on the glass of the front door and waited. In seconds, Wren was unlocking and opening it.

"Glad you could make it over here. How did it go with the parents?"

I rolled my neck and shoulders, feeling tense after a long day. "Not as helpful as I'd hoped but they did seem to think Aleigha might have been afraid of something."

"Something as in...?"

"That's about all I got." I shrugged in resignation. "I did learn that Aleigha was adopted, so there's that."

Wren twisted his face in an expression of disbelief and indignation. "You didn't already know that, Miss Sleuth? It was major news."

"I don't exactly read the *Landsfield Ridge Gazette*, Wren." I stifled a yawn. It had been a long day and I was beginning to feel the strain.

He shook his head and walked around the circulation desk. He clicked his mouse a few times to wake up the computer and typed something in. "That's not what I mean. It made national headlines. Aleigha's rescue and adoption was a big story at the time. Were you living under a rock?"

"I was in Afghanistan," I deadpanned.

His clicking finger froze over the mouse. "Oh. Well. Um, thank you for your—"

"Please don't 'thank you for your service' me. It's awkward, no matter what."

"Duly noted," he nodded and looked back at the screen. "See? Right here. In *USA Today*."

I looked at the screen, which was pulled up to the *USA Today* archives. Sure enough, there was little Aleigha. The photograph was definitely meant to tug at your heartstrings. A toddler being raised from the rubble of her home, crying in the arms of a relief worker. The headline read, "Rescued Orphan Adopted by Small-Town Surgeon." I cringed at the white savior theme running through the article.

"So, she wasn't just popular in town. She was basically famous."

Wren wriggled his hands in an offhand gesture. "I don't know. This was a while back and everyone has short attention spans nowadays. The library gets emptier and emptier every year."

"Still, we can't discount someone who followed her story."

He scratched his head and gave a half-hearted shrug. "It's not impossible. But we haven't had any media coverage on the story in years. It's just... unlikely. Oh! Let me show you the account I found."

I then remembered the reason I had met Wren here in the first place. "Right, the second instagram account?"

He clicked away from the *USA Today* page and pulled up a new tab. The social media account he brought up didn't seem to throw up any red flags so I looked over to Wren.

"Am I missing something? This seems like a perfectly normal instagram page."

He shook his head and clicked through the pictures. "At surface level, yes. But I began to notice that there isn't a single picture of her in any of her clubs or teams. They're all flattering photos, even some bikini pics." He cleared his throat, clearly uncomfortable with the topic. "Compared to her other account, this one is obviously being utilized to emphasize her physical qualities."

"This is the account she hides from her parents that has borderline racy photos, you mean. Maybe this is what the girls were talking about." I took the mouse from his hand and began scrolling. Sure enough, the photos were designed to be as flattering as possible. No sport or club photos. Nothing of her personality.

"Exactly. And what's better, I tried logging in. She has a fairly easy password reset question. Happen to know her dog's name?"

I searched my memory and came up empty. "I don't actually. But I bet I can find out."

········

The drive back home found me buzzing with excitement. I couldn't help the nervous energy running through my body. Finding a fascinating case was always something that got my blood pumping and my brain buzzing. This was like a fix for a starving addict.

I could sense that I was getting close to something. What, I wasn't sure. I just had to keep pursuing it, the chief's warnings be damned.

As I pulled into my driveway, though, my excitement faded. There was something amiss. Years of military training had taught me to be aware of my surroundings and I'd developed something of a sixth sense. I looked through my windows and windshield, hoping to find an obvious sign of something unusual but nothing jumped out at me.

Then I saw it. Something was painted on the door. I turned off the car and grabbed the taser in my purse. One can never be too cautious in moments like this. I was confident I could handle myself but as the Morgenstern's had said, it was best to use all resources at your disposal.

Taking a deep breath, I exited the car and walked toward the door. I gasped slightly as I saw the words scrawled there.

GIVE UP.

Chapter 6

I stared at the message on my door that night, noticing the tackiness of the paint on the poor little parsonage. It couldn't have been there for more than 30 minutes. For a fleeting moment, I had considered calling it into the police. But they weren't exactly my biggest fans and there was no proof that this came from someone involved with the disappearance. At the rate this investigation was going, it could be any number of disgruntled townspeople. I sighed and sent a text to the owners of the house alerting them of the incident.

As I looked at the warning sign, something occurred to me. I ran into the kitchen and grabbed a butter knife and ziploc bag. I decided to keep a sample of the paint for my investigation. *Couldn't hurt, besides, it's as good a lead as any.* I carefully placed the paint sample in the bag and realized that it was cellulose based. Very common among body shops when detailing cars, a tip I'd picked up from a friendly enough source during a former case.

·····•·•····

I sipped my coffee the next morning (no visit to Lili's after the previous day's snafu) and sat down in the rocking chair on the porch. As soon as I sat down, my phone chimed. A text from Evelyn. I had reached out to her late the night before regarding the name of the family dog.

Evelyn: Bella.

I silently thanked the powers that be that she didn't ask me why I needed the information. The fog of fear and grief hung thick over her mind—I assumed—and she probably answered without thinking it through. Another message came through soon after.

Evelyn: Any news?

I quickly typed back a response, letting her know that I had a few leads but I wasn't sure if they amounted to anything yet. I would reach out to her when I had a better idea of what those meant. Content with my response, I tucked my phone back into my pocket and surveyed the neighborhood, wondering if one of my neighbors had marked my door.

Surprisingly, this wasn't the first time I'd been warned to back off. I had received several threatening letters that my law firm and the police department both had copies of, filed away somewhere. Written by those 'wronged' by my investigations. Still, this one seemed personal, written right on the door of the house in which I was staying. A shudder ran through me. After a few moments of thought, I shook it off and pulled out my phone again, this time to text Wren. We had a strong lead and I'd be damned if this message would warn me off the trail.

Me: Bella.

Wren: What?

Me: The dog's name.

Wren: On it!

I waited a beat before replying. Even though it might not amount to much, I figured I might as well give it a shot.

Me: Know anything about paint?

·····•·····

The library was practically empty on that Monday afternoon. I noticed a homeless woman seated at one of the computers but save for her presence, it was just me and Wren. We huddled around the desktop at the circulation desk, prepared to unveil the latest part of the mystery. The note on my door was still fresh in my mind but I figured we could hold off for now. There were more pressing leads to pursue at the moment.

With the password reset answer at our disposal, we could log into the secondary instagram account, and hopefully glean something from the contents—messages sent, posts liked—anything that could lead us in the right direction.

"And we're in. I set the password to 'Welcome123.'" Wren said, as he typed in the login information.

"Very secure password. How very 'hacker' of you." I nudged his shoulder with mine playfully, only to see a blush creep up his face. *Whoops*. "So, first I think we should check the messages."

"Fair enough," Wren said, having composed himself some-what. He clicked on the app's inbox and a wall of messages appeared. "Huh, she's been quite busy lately. Looks like she's messaged half the town."

I pointed at the more recent messages. "Let's look at some of the latest stuff. There's likely to be a clue as to her last steps."

"Yes, Sir," he joked, clicking on the top message. The screen name read mwest2005. When he opened up the string of messages, I was surprised to find an entire conversation. Wren scrolled up to find where it all began. Surprisingly, not long ago. Maybe two weeks back. What I gleaned from the early messages were simple flirtation and general kid shenanigans. As we began to scroll through, we found nothing that would explain a sudden disappearance. No threats. No talk of anything troubling.

"Wait, hold on." I grabbed the mouse from Wren's hand and scrolled down to the latest messages. "About a week ago, she began asking him questions. About his father?"

Wren slapped his forehead. "Of course. Mwest must be Michael Westenberg."

"Westenberg as in Mayor Westenberg?"

"Michael is his son. Around the same age as Aleigha, I believe. But what would she want to know about Frederick?"

I scrolled through the remaining messages. "It looks like she was asking about his early career. When he became mayor, what kind of dad he was... Honestly, the litany of questions is kind of long."

"No wonder he ghosted her."

"What?"

Wren pointed at the screen. "The last few messages. She reached out trying to get him to respond and there's nothing from his side. Maybe things got too weird for him."

I chewed on my lip and considered the messages. "This is weird, right? I don't know many teenage girls who are that interested in how someone came to be mayor."

"Agreed," Wren muttered, scanning through the rest of the messages. "There are a ton of other conversations. It might take a while to go through them. Want me to order us some coffee and food so we're fueled up to get started?"

That actually sounded amazing but I worried that Wren would get the wrong idea. He was a sweet guy and I didn't want to lead him on. I was used to male attention, it wasn't like I was blind to my appearance. I knew I was well-educated and attractive, but it just tended to make things more complicated. *I have to find a way to let him down easily.*

"Actually, I think we should split our efforts again. I'll go talk to Michael Westenberg, you see if there are any other messages of importance here. And if it's not too much..." I hesitated as I rummaged through my bag. "Here's the paint sample I texted you about, could you possibly see what you can find out about it?"

I watched as Wren visibly deflated. It wasn't fun turning him down, I could tell that he was beginning to show interest. But in the short time I'd be here notwithstanding, I just didn't have the time for romantic entanglements of any kind. In fact, I hadn't for a long time.

"Sure thing. I'll do some deep diving. You go see what Michael knows. School is out by now so he should be at football practice."

I raised an eyebrow. "You have a copy of his schedule?"

Wren shrugged, looking sheepish. "Everyone knows everyone. He's the second-string receiver on the high school team. And they usually practice after school."

The answer made me sad. Here was Wren, clearly involved in the town, still seen as an outsider in his own home. The small town had its outward charm, but there was a dark side lurking just underneath.

"I'll head that way." I was prepared to dart out the door when I saw the dejected look on Wren's face. It melted something in me that had been frozen for a while. "Hey, it's not you."

He looked up, a look of soft confusion. "What isn't?"

I frowned and placed my bag down on the circulation desk. "This town," I hesitated a moment. "And me."

Wren said nothing, waiting for me to elaborate. I scrambled to organize my thoughts. "This town has its issues that have nothing to do with someone who moved here as a kid. If you ask me, it's a toxic way of life masquerading as hometown pride."

"And you?" It seemed like it almost pained him to ask.

I sighed and ran my hand through my hair, taking a moment to lean against the desk. "I'm not interested but it's not you. It's me. Which sounds like bullshit. But the truth is, I haven't really had much interest in anyone."

Wren seemed to consider that for a few moments. Finally, he looked up at me, "You deserve not to be alone, you know."

The vulnerability and earnestness in his expression caught me off-guard. I wasn't used to people looking out for me. I had always been fiercely independent, determined to make my way in the world alone. It was a nice reminder that maybe I didn't always have to have my guard up. "Thanks, Wren. I appreciate that." Before the moment became awkward, I grabbed my bag off the desk again and began rummaging around for my keys. "Which way is the high school?"

·····•·•·····

The football team's practice was winding down when I arrived. I hovered along the outside of the fence for a while, simply watching. I wasn't much for sports but it seemed like they were fairly decent. Championship banners were hung by the scoreboard and the coach looked rather official in his team windbreaker, giving pep talks to the players as they did their cooldown stretches.

I took a moment to observe the practice. In a town like this, sports are often a significant unifier. The games were a draw for the townsfolk, allowing them to enthusiastically represent their small town pride. At least, in every movie that I'd ever watched featuring a small town.

As the players broke for water, I bided my time by checking my phone. No new texts. No news was never good news when it came to mysteries. It just meant frustration. I clicked over to my browser and searched Michael's name. Nothing came up except a locked down Facebook page. Cursing, I gave up and clicked back out. *Looks like I'm going in blind.*

The team began to meander out of the practice area and I saw it as my opportunity. I spotted Michael Westenberg heading out, a backpack slung over his shoulder. Trying not to seem too eager, I placed my phone back in my pocket and walked toward him slowly. "You guys seem to be a pretty strong team," I said as I approached. I was hoping the passive comment would drop his guard. I didn't need another angry townsperson calling the police department.

He narrowed his eyes, less distrustful and more like he was struggling to make me out. I wondered fleetingly whether the kid needed glasses.

"I'm sorry, who are you?"

I kept my hands in my pockets. "A friend of the Morgenstern's. I was hoping maybe you'd be willing to talk with me."

"About what, exactly?" He adjusted the strap of his bag on his shoulder.

"About Aleigha. It seems like you guys got close for a while."

He eyed me suspiciously. "What do you mean by that?"

"We have uncovered a history of messages between the two of you. Seemed pretty flirtatious."

He rolled his eyes and snorted in derision. "Yeah, at first. She was being all cutesy, coming on real strong and it felt good, ya know? But then she started asking weird questions."

"About your family."

His lips pursed for a moment. "Yeah, about my dad. She was probably just interested in the damn scholarship he awards every year. Had nothing to do with me, but it's whatever." The tone of his voice told me that it was far from 'whatever' to him.

"Scholarship?"

"Yeah, there's a scholarship that my dad is on the board for. They decide which student gets it each year. She must have wanted it bad because she's starting early. She won't even be eligible until her senior year and she's just a sophomore."

I considered this new information. While it was possible Aleigha wanted that scholarship, it seemed unlikely she would go about it this way. Still, I hardly remembered what it was like to be a teenager. And the world has changed a lot since then. "So, she just wanted to know about your father?"

"Yeah, it was weird. She wanted to know all kinds of stuff about his career and whatnot. What he did in law enforcement. Maybe she wanted to cozy on up to him, pretend like she cared about his career before politics. I don't know."

I chewed on my lip. It was interesting that she seemed so intent on nabbing a scholarship she wasn't yet eligible for. For the life of me, though, I couldn't see how that fit into the puzzle.

Michael shifted uncomfortably in place. "Look. I don't like what she did. But I still hope she comes home safe and sound, okay? I'm not a monster."

I softened at that. He may have been a moody teenager, but he didn't seem like he was capable of being involved. His pride was just wounded at the ulterior motives of the girl he had shown interest in. I could relate, on some level.

"Of course not, I replied. "We all want to see Aleigha come home but you must understand we have to follow all clues... no matter where they lead. Speaking of which, I was wondering if you had heard anything about any vandals in town?"

Michael darted his eyes over to his teammates who were all heading home. "Not really, this isn't that kind of town."

"Well, thank you for your time." I didn't know if this conversation had really led anywhere of value but at least it marked another dead end off the list.

Still, something was bothering me about the whole thing. I felt like I was missing something but for the life of me, couldn't pinpoint what that was. It would continue to bug me until I could put the pieces in the correct place.

As I walked back to my car, I dodged the suspicious looks coming from Michael's teammates. I had grown accustomed to the distrust but it was still uncomfortable to feel it so intensely. I did my best to ignore the eyes burning a hole in the back of my head as I climbed into my Saturn and put the car into drive.

I stayed there for a few moments, mulling over the information that Michael had given me. Could Aleigha have wanted to get out of town? I thought back to what Aleigha's parents had said about her double checking the doors at night. Maybe there was something she was trying to get away from. But what?

My reverie was interrupted by my phone buzzing in my pocket. I hesitated, wanting to follow my train of thought to a conclusion. The buzzing was making it hard to focus, though, so I pulled it out. Wren's caller ID flashed on the screen. I answered, hoping for some more direction.

"What have you got?" I winced at my lack of pleasantries. I was always too brusque. Wren didn't seem to mind.

"A lot. I don't think this profile belongs to Aleigha."

"Come again?"

"It's a catfish. Aleigha didn't create this profile."

Chapter 7

I threw open the doors of the library in unbridled enthusiasm. "Explain."

Wren's head popped up from where he'd been reshelving books. His face split into a grin and he carried the remainder of the books over to the desk. "The key was going through the older messages and comparing them to the other profile we found for Aleigha."

He beckoned me forward to meet him behind the desk. As I got closer, I could see tabs were already open, displaying both social media pages.

"Okay, so I looked into the older messages and found something really interesting. First of all, her grammar."

"Her grammar?" I asked doubtfully.

"Yeah, it sounds like a small thing but everyone has a way they talk or write on social media. The messages and post captions didn't match the grammar I was seeing on the other profile. Little things, but they piqued my interest. And the people she was talking to don't match her friends list on the other profile. In fact, it seems entirely random. Lili is on here, as well as several other prominent members of the community."

"So, what does that mean?"

"I highly believe this profile is a catfish. Aleigha was never running it. We have an impostor in our midst, it would seem."

I blew out a long breath. "So, one lead closes, opening another one. Any idea who might be the catfish?"

Wren shrugged, a little dejectedly. "Unfortunately, I wasn't able to determine that. The email address that's attached to the account gives no clues to an identity and it doesn't look like they ever revealed themselves." He brightened slightly. "*But*, I think the best thing to do is start with the first person they contacted."

"Why is that important?"

Wren scrolled further down the page and clicked on the message. "Well, for starters. It's the earliest message by far. The other messages didn't start until a month later. And secondly, the, uh... messages are enlightening."

"Do tell."

"She was messaging Preston Scott. Really flirty stuff."

I frowned, not seeing the significance. "So, the catfish was catfishing. What's so unusual about that?"

Wren leaned back in his chair and steepled his fingers. "Preston Scott—boyfriend of one Margery Morgenstern. At the time, anyway. I think they've since broken up. No great loss for Margery, apparently."

"My eyes widened. "The sister?"

He nodded, turning back to the messages. "The very same. And judging from the messages the boyfriend was sending, she had a bit of trouble in paradise. He was not exactly the faithful sort."

"And he thought this was Margery's sister? That's sick."

Wren shrugged. "Teenage hormones, douchebag culture. Take your pick. The fact is, cheating is kind of commonplace in this town. There's a running joke that everyone goes to school together, dates everyone, cheats, grows up, marries, rinse, repeat."

"Ew."

"I know. It's not exactly advertised in our brochure. But it is what it is."

I read some of the messages over Wren's shoulder and frowned. "These messages drop off, just like the ones with Michael. Perhaps our catfish got cold feet." I reached the end of the message thread and sighed, "Right around the time Preston suggested a midnight tryst. What a winner."

"Must've scared the catfish off," Wren said. "Not actually being Aleigha and all."

"Right," I muttered, trying to make the pieces fit. "Seems like a weird redirect, though. Right? Why pursue Preston and then later switch gears into asking about the Westenberg family?"

"That is the question. I think figuring that out might help give us an idea of who we're dealing with."

I considered everything we had learned so far. Pulling a legal pad and pen out of my bag, I began jotting down the clues I'd gathered. "Okay, so we have a catfish. A catfish interested in Margery's boyfriend and the Westenberg family."

"Which is an interesting combo."

"Why do you say that?" I asked, chewing on the end of my pen. It was a bad habit I'd never really been able to break.

"The Westenbergs are like Landsfield Ridge royalty. Well, the remaining Westenbergs. Michael's mother, Sophia, passed away a few years ago. But Preston? I'm not trying to be cruel but the kid has been a bit of a burnout for a while. In and out of juvie, drug use, bad grades. Honestly, I never really understood what Margery saw in him."

"Teenage hormones. Douchebag culture. Take your pick," I repeated back to him. "Teenagers aren't exactly known for picking the good ones." I thought back to my own teenage exploits and shuddered slightly. Hindsight is a hell of a thing.

"Well, whatever was happening with this profile, it seems like Preston was the original target. So maybe it's best you check with him as your next step?"

I nodded, considering my options. "Well, it's starting to get late in the day but I can ask the Morgenstern's for his contact information. I'll call him tomorrow. What did you find out about the paint sample?"

"Well," Wren started, "I wasn't really sure where to start, so I went over to the auto shop to ask if anyone there could help us out."

"And?"

Wren looked at me and smirked. "And... I spoke to George. He told me that the paint sample you gave me is the same type that Michael purchased to detail his car not long ago."

"So you think the mayor's son tagged the house? It seems like a pretty common color, so how do you know it's him?"

"You're right, it is a common color and there are many cars around here with the same profile." Wren replied, "but it's something."

I took a beat to let this new information sink in. "I think I might call it a night here."

Wren nodded with an expression of concern. "You are kind of running yourself ragged. Why did you come out here, anyway? Tell me it wasn't supposed to be a vacation."

I grinned sheepishly at him. "Guilty."

He sighed. "Just try to get some rest tonight, okay? Do something relaxing. Something more... vacation-like."

I laughed, but again, I found myself warmed at the thought of someone who felt the need to look out for me. I was always such an intimidating presence, people rarely thought it necessary. It could get lonely. "Librarian's orders. I got it. Have a good night, Wren. Stay safe."

"You too," he said with a heaviness. Maybe Wren wasn't immune to the trepidation felt by the town. And maybe that was for the best. After all, Aleigha had been afraid of something, hadn't she?

······•··•·····

On the drive home, I took in the town through my windshield. It was easier to see the sinister side now that the sun was setting—and with the knowledge I'd managed to glean so far.

As I drew to a stop at the town's only stop light, I took a deep breath and let it out. Wren had been right, damn him. This trip had been meant as a getaway. A breather from all the work I'd been buried under for months. And here I was, chasing a mystery. I couldn't walk away from it but I could take the night to relax.

Considering all this, I suddenly noticed something out of the corner of my eye. Another car had stopped behind me. I went back through my memory and realized I had seen it several times during my drive. *Surely they aren't following me*. In a town this small, it was common for people to take similar routes.

Still, the hairs on the back of my neck stood up. Call it intuition. Call it a spidey sense. Something seemed off; I felt uneasy. I quickly picked up my phone from the center console and took a couple of photos to examine later. *That's got to be a coincidence*, I thought. As the light turned green, I drove toward the Airbnb, white knuckling the steering wheel. As the car continued to stay somewhat back and on the same route, my heart rate sped up a bit. It had all the signs of a tail but I still couldn't be completely certain.

As I finally turned onto the street that housed the Airbnb, I held my breath and reached around for my pepper spray. But the car kept going, not making the turn. I let out my breath and relaxed slightly. I pulled into the driveway and sat back, recovering my faculties.

Am I being paranoid? Or is someone sending another message?

The question swirled in my brain as I got out of my car. My fight or flight successfully heightened, I wondered how I'd be able to wind down for the night. I swiftly made my way into the house and double checked the lock. After doing a quick perimeter check, I ascertained that all the windows and doors were still locked. I could breathe easier.

I tossed my bag onto the cozy little couch when I re-entered the living room and rolled my shoulders. Tension had built up in them and tonight was supposed to be about relaxing. *You're overreacting*, I told myself. *Take some time for yourself.*

I wandered into the small, old-fashioned kitchen. Passing up the coffee maker, I headed to where I'd stashed the wine I had brought with me.

A nice Cloudy Bay sparkling wine from New Zealand, perfect for a night to unwind. I popped the cork and poured myself a generous glass. I watched as the bubbles swirled in the glass for a moment, letting my rattled nerves calm.

I took my alcohol and a bag of chocolate covered pretzels to the living room, placing them on the low coffee table. *Now for something to do with myself.* Anime was always an option. But the excitement of the shows seemed like a bit too much for me. I wandered over to the bookcase along the far wall and perused the shelves.

I traced my fingers along the spines of the books. There was a wide variety ranging from old fantasy paperbacks to newer theology commentaries. It was an interesting mix and made me start to wonder about the family that lived here. I'd been told it was a parsonage, so clearly, it was a preacher's family. That explained the theology volumes. But what were they like? Had they lived here their whole lives or were they outsiders like Wren?

I shook myself out of my reverie and finally settled on a beat-up paperback of *The Fellowship of the Ring*. It was a book my father often read to me as a child. It brought back warm memories of comfort and safety. Plucking it off the shelf, I settled back onto the couch with my refreshments. I sunk into the couch and sighed, pulling a crocheted blanket around me.

Tonight was about vacation. Tonight was about recharging. Tomorrow, the search for Aleigha would continue. *And, I will investigate those photos,* I thought to myself.

·····•·•·····

"Thank you for your help," I said into the phone as Evelyn began to sniffle again. She had supplied me with the number for Preston Scott but was clearly still struggling. I had spent the last five minutes trying to politely excuse myself from the phone call.

I looked back at Wren who was waiting behind the circulation desk, eager to hear what I had gleaned from the family. It seemed he was getting lax about the cell phone policy in the library. I was grateful.

"So?"

"So, I have contact information for Preston Scott. I'll be able to call him in about," I checked my watch, "fifteen minutes. School is out, but I want to give it some time in case he gets held up."

Wren cracked his knuckles. "Well then, that gives me some time to fill you in on what I've discovered from these messages. I spent most of last night reading through all the conversations thoroughly. And it seems that Michael was not the only one she asked about the Westenberg patriarch."

"Really? That's strange."

"Tell me about it. It was like she was writing a book on the guy. She also asked a few questions that might interest you."

I moved closer to the computer. "Like what?"

Wren scratched his head and looked a little sheepish. "Well, I might have been a bit too hasty in one of my earlier assessments."

"Meaning?"

He scrolled through the messages quickly. "I mean, they were also asking about other people's movements and remembrances of two thousand three."

I drew in a quick breath. "The year of the cold case."

He snapped and pointed at me. "Exactly. The cases might be connected after all. It just doesn't make any sense. It was way too long ago to have any real connection, surely? But faux Aleigha seemed very interested in details surrounding the case. Their interest in the beloved mayor might mean they had landed on a suspect."

I chewed on my bottom lip and tapped a pen against the desk. "Anything else about him in those messages?"

He grinned, his chest puffing out a bit. "Glad you asked. It looks like they targeted a few of the town gossips. Those who might be more willing to open up about anything untoward.

One particular chatterbox, Tina Trettin, had a lot to say about the mayor's romantic entanglements."

"Wasn't he married?"

"He was. For quite some time. But according to this little birdie, there were rumors about his... indiscretions."

"Affairs, you mean." I felt my heart beat a little faster. This was definitely a piece to the puzzle, though I wasn't quite sure where it fit just yet.

"Yep, it seems our favorite mayor had trouble keeping it in his pants during his marriage. According to Miss Trettin, Sophia had no idea. But I don't know. In a town this small..."

I nodded. "Well, that gives us a pretty solid lead but we're still flying blind until we identify this catfish and figure out why they are so interested in such an old case."

"Get any other leads?" Wren asked eagerly; it seemed the bug for crime solving had settled within him as well.

"Well..." I began, "I noticed this car following me home last night, or, at least I thought it was." I tapped my phone a few times, bringing up the photos I took to show him. "I've seen it around but being such a small town, I'm not sure what to make of it."

"Why don't you send those to me and I can look into it while you're talking to Preston? That way we can follow two leads at once."

That didn't sound like a bad idea. Glancing down at my phone, I realized the 15 minutes I had given Preston were up. "Be right back, I'm going to give another philanderer a call. You should receive those pics any minute."

Wren nodded and started to head for the circulation cart. "I have some reshelving to do anyway but I will look into those once I finish this up. Let me know what you find out."

I stepped out of the library and into the brisk air. The air was stirring in a way that told me it was threatening rain, something not unexpected in Northern California this time of year. The only surprise was that it had taken this long for the downpour to occur.

Hands shaking with anticipation, I dialed the number that Evelyn had provided: Preston's cell phone number. As the call connected, I listened to it ring. And ring. And ring. When I was about to give up on the call entirely (everyone has caller ID these days), I finally heard someone pick up.

"Who is this?" The voice sounded sharp, with a touch of annoyance.

"Hi, Preston. This is a friend of the Morgenstern family. I was wondering if we could talk."

There was such a long silence that I almost thought he'd hung up on me. Finally, there was a sigh. "What do you want to know?" The sharp edge of his voice had taken on a new harshness, like a cornered animal. Which was good for my purposes.

"Well, I found a secondary profile page for Aleigha and it seems you exchanged messages with the account."

Preston snorted. "Oh, right. That. I don't know what that has to do with Aleigha's disappearance unless her sister is more psycho than I thought."

I had not been expecting that. *Margery? How does she factor into this mess?* I took a beat to think about my next question. There was no need to rush this and I had a feeling that Preston would be a valuable fount of knowledge. "What does Margery have to do with this?"

Preston sighed and let out a humorless laugh. "Because Margery was the catfish."

Chapter 8

I didn't know how to respond to this revelation. *Margery had been masquerading as her sister?* I cleared my throat, giving myself a second to collect myself. "How do you know?"

"Look, Margery is all right and all. But she's also super intense and just so goody two shoes. Her sister though? Smoke show. So when she started to send me messages, I responded, as any guy with a pulse would. Anyway, the messages tapered off and suddenly Margery is dumping me. It doesn't take Elon Musk to put the pieces together."

That tracked. Margery had clearly been insecure about her sister's popularity. Maybe she had suspected disloyalty in her boyfriend and thought to put it to the test. That still left the question as to why her activities had changed so abruptly.

"Did she ever come out and admit to being the catfish?" I asked, hoping that maybe the rest of the story would shed some light on the situation.

A wry laugh escaped him. "Nah, she'd never admit to underhanded bullshit like that. But I knew. She kept talking about her sister when she broke up with me."

"Did she say anything else?" I thought maybe I was pressing my luck. Preston Scott didn't exactly seem like the most trustworthy person. I couldn't see someone as savvy as Margery expressing her future plans to him after unceremoniously dumping him.

"Oh, she said plenty. Called me every name in the book."

"I mean about anything not regarding your... relationship."

"Or lack thereof? Nah, she just went off on me. I thought it was weird she kept the catfish account up but I figured that was none of my business. The bitch can do whatever crazy shit she wants."

Wren had been right. This guy was clearly no winner and Margery really had no business dating him. It seemed like she had dodged a particularly douchey bullet with this one. "Well, thank you for your time, Preston. This conversation has been enlightening." *In more ways than one.*

"Yeah, whatever," he said, before unceremoniously ending the call. What a guy.

I stood there for a moment staring at my phone. *So, Margery had been the mysterious catfish.* This changed everything. Could it be possible that Margery's exploits had something to do with Aleigha's disappearance? I vaguely wondered about the stones she had been kicking up. Surely someone had taken notice.

With a sigh, I pocketed my phone and observed the garden surrounding the pathway to the library. Such beauty in such an ugly place. It seemed like the more I uncovered, the more I realized this town was poisonous. Not just to outsiders like Wren, but to everyone. The small town charm was just a shiny veneer on a darker reality.

I kicked at some dirt, dismayed at this realization. This place was supposed to be somewhere I could go to forget the craziness of big city life. But apparently it had its own brand of crazy.

Finally coming to terms with everything that I had just un-covered, I headed back into the library, feeling a wall of heat hit me as the doors opened.

"So?" Wren hadn't even made any pretense of working while I was on the phone. He was sitting behind the circulation desk, tapping a pen against the wood. His anticipation was nearly palpable.

"It looks like I have the identity of our catfish. Margery Morgenstern."

Wren's face contorted into an expression of shock. "No. Really? She doesn't seem the type."

I shrugged and settled in the seat across from him. "Well, it looks like it started as a test of her boyfriend's loyalty. One he obviously failed. But for some reason, it didn't end there. I just need to figure out why."

Wren scratched at his thinning hair and blew out a deep breath. "Well, I hate to say it but I think your only option is to try talking to Margery again."

"Because that went so well last time."

"Yeah, but this time, you have Evelyn and Matthew on your side. Margery probably got a stern talking-to and might be a bit more willing to talk to you now."

I ground my teeth. Wren definitely had a point. The parents of young Margery had seemed appalled at her behavior and she had probably received an earful. It might make it more likely that she would speak with me. Still, it made it difficult to earn her trust completely. Finally, I shook my head, decision made. "Screw it. You're right. This might be the chance to get some actual answers. I'll head up there now."

"Before you go, I searched Michael's social media accounts for a match to the car and found one post on his Instagram of a BMW that looked promising—an early birthday present—probably from his father. Unfortunately the paint color was the only similarity."

"So it was just a coincidence, then." I was about to head out the door without a second thought but I paused. "Thank you, by the way, I don't think I've said it enough but your work on the social media accounts and your knowledge of the town have helped me immensely."

I realized, again, that I had been treating him as an assistant. I had a habit of categorizing people. It kept me somewhat closed off, I knew. Something that my father would be dismayed to find had come to pass. He had always been an open book and treated no one as a stranger. Wren, though, had made me question the way I viewed the world and people in it.

Wren, this town, it was all a mess of dichotomies. The Straight A catfish, the outsider with the insider knowledge, the secrets that hid behind smiles. It was a case that made you stop and take stock.

Wren grinned bashfully and scratched his head. "It was nothing, really."

"No, it was great and I appreciate it. We're going to bring Aleigha home. And it will be because of you."

If Wren was grinning before, he was beaming now. His whole countenance lit up with the shred of recognition that I'd given him. God, I hoped he could get out of this town some day.

"Thanks, Maya. I just want to do my part."

I nodded, suddenly uncomfortable with this vulnerability. I cleared my throat and stood up a little straighter, shaking off the awkward aftermath of my gratitude. "So, uh, I guess I'll head up to the Morgenstern's now."

Wren nodded, seeming to catch on to my discomfort. He tried to dim his smile but I could see the twitching in his lips that betrayed him. "Yeah, of course. Let me know what you find out."

I gave him a warm smile before departing the library. On the way to my car, I texted Evelyn letting her know that I would be dropping in. After a brief pause I also let her know I was hoping to speak with Margery.

··············

Arriving outside the Morgenstern estate, I was once again blown away by their evident affluence. A family like this would be royalty in a small town. No wonder the entire town got involved in the search—off to chase a missing princess.

I walked up the front drive and onto the porch, noting that Evelyn wasn't waiting at the screen door this time. I knocked lightly on the door and to my surprise, Margery answered. Her face was set in an expression of petulance and her eyes were narrowed.

"Mom said you wanted to talk to me again."

I wasted less time on trying to appear disarming. That ship had sailed and I knew Margery had serious answers. "Yes, Margery. We need to talk about the fake Instagram page you've been running in your sister's name."

The effect was immediate. Margery's face blanched and I could see wheels turning in her head. I highly suspected she wanted to slam that door right in my face but I held all the cards. "Come in," she finally said, holding the door open for me.

Margery didn't make any pleasantries as she walked me up to her room. Apparently she didn't see the point in pleasant chit-chat anymore, either. The stomps of her shoes against the stairs let me know she wasn't all too pleased I had finally seen through her ruse. When we got to her room, Margery wordlessly gestured to the bed before plopping down in her computer chair. I took a seat, staring down the stone faced expression Margery gave me.

"So," I started.

"So," Margery parroted. "You think you know something."

I held up my hands in a gesture of innocence. "Look, I'm not assuming anything here. We have pretty substantial evidence that points to you as being the one running that secondary account. We just want to know why."

Margery's closed-off expression wavered and I could see tears glisten in her eyes for a moment before she blinked them away. "Do you have any idea what it's like to be in someone's shadow? She's my *little* sister and yet, she's the one everyone knows. She's the one everyone wanted to be around. She's so beautiful and her story so tragic, how are you supposed to measure up to that?" The tears were back by the end of her speech and streaming down her face.

I sighed, suddenly feeling a wave of overwhelming sympathy. I couldn't relate to her struggle, not having any siblings. But I could see what that burden had done to her. "I just need to know why you made that page, Margery. It could be really important in finding out what happened."

Margery sniffled and rubbed at her nose with her sweater's sleeve. "It was so stupid."

"What was?"

She sighed and fiddled with her sleeves in her lap. "The reason I started it. I could tell that Preston was paying extra attention to my sister when he came over. I got suspicious. I just wanted to see—" She broke off into a ragged sob.

I nodded and clasped my hands together. "I'm really sorry. In my experience, high school romances are rarely happily ever after. But that must have been awful."

She didn't say anything, just continued to sniffle, though I saw her nodding along.

"But Margery, if it was just about Preston... then why did you keep it up? Why were you," I searched for the words, "investigating the town?"

Margery looked up, her face a mask of surprise. "You... you saw that too?"

"I did. Why were you using a fake account of your sister to go poking around?"

She sighed and wiped some of the tears and snot off of her face. "Because people *like* Aleigha. I'm just the weird older sister. I thought they'd be more interested in talking to her." She turned in her chair and grabbed a folder which she handed to me.

I flipped it open to find an informational pamphlet about a scholarship. *Had this all been about a scholarship, after all?*

"Stanford has a special scholarship for investigative journalism. I started with a deep dive into the school budget but come on, it's *Stanford*. I wanted to do something... bigger."

"Which is when you thought of the town cold case."

She almost seemed to get excited. "Yes! Exactly. That was my story. I knew it made no sense that some random drifter did it, ya know? That's always the story we tell ourselves."

So apparently Wren isn't the only one who sees through the town line.

She continued in a rush, "I started looking into it and it seemed like the police did a bang-up job of botching the case. Evidence was contaminated or never submitted."

"How do you know all this? It wasn't in the messages."

At this, Margery blushed. "A true investigator never reveals her sources."

I leveled her with a stone cold gaze. "Margery, I'm an attorney and I feel like I'm catching a whiff of something illegal. Spill now, and maybe I'll look the other way."

The reaction was instantaneous. Her eyes widened and she scrambled for another file folder on her desk. "I might have, sort of, slipped into the police station after hours."

"You broke into a police station."

"Yes?"

I opened the file and sighed, rubbing at my temples. "And stole the cold case files. Margery, do you have any idea how illegal and dangerous all of this was?"

"I know! I know! I just wanted that scholarship. I wanted to get away from here so badly. I thought this story was the key. I—I sort of got caught up in it." She looked miserable at the thought. "It wasn't supposed to get so out of control."

I bit back whatever response had been bubbling at my lips. "I understand that. So the messages—they were to mine for information on your potential suspects."

She nodded, "I thought, ya know, more people like my sister. They trust her. People open up to her in restaurant bathrooms, for god's sake."

I swallowed, feeling a tightness in my chest. "Margery, you were messing around in something extremely dangerous. In your sister's name. This is something we should have known from the beginning. It could have saved us a lot of time." I was trying not to be too harsh, but I couldn't fathom the irresponsible measures she had taken.

The tears came back yet again. "I know! I know. I wanted to say something but my parents would *kill* me."

"Really, Margery. Kill you? They love you."

"THEY LOVE *HER.*"

I was stunned at the venom in her words. The anger, the resentment, the sadness. A mixture that would make anyone do some ill-advised things.

The tears and snot were now coming down in a freefall. "Have you ever heard the way they talk about her? Their *miracle* child. Because their first one just wasn't enough!" She tried to catch her breath in a ragged gasp. "I didn't know if it was relevant and I didn't, didn't," she hiccupped. "I didn't want to lose their love."

I considered getting up to comfort the girl but I sat on the bed, stunned by the flood of emotion. I had seen the mantle. I had heard the way the Morgenstern parents talked about Aleigha. I could see how Margery felt trapped in her own web.

"Margery," I said softly, trying to break her out of her emotional meltdown. "Margery, I think the killer from the cold case is someone in this town. And I think they came after your sister because of what they thought she knew."

Margery nodded miserably. "I don't even have anything concrete. Just a theory. A fairly solid one, but I don't know if it would be enough to put anyone away."

I pondered this. "But in a town this small, even a hint of this scandal could bring someone to ruin. The rumor mill is law around here. So think, Margery. Who were you closing in on?"

Her eyes widened as she looked at me. "It's just a theory."

"Margery, the time for waffling on this is over. I need that name."

"Frederick Westenberg," she told me. "The mayor. I think he killed the Rawley girl back in two thousand three to cover up his affair with her."

Chapter 9

I sat on the edge of the bed, stunned at her pronouncement. Sure, the questions about the family had definitely meant something. It wasn't completely surprising to hear that she suspected Mayor Westenberg of being the murderer. However, there was still necessary evidence. Something of which we had very little.

"What makes you say it was Mayor Westenberg, Margery?"

She wiped at the tears on her face and gestured toward the file. "It's all in there. He clearly botched the investigation. I've read about him in the newspaper. He was a great cop. Heralded as a hero more than once. So why look the other way unless he had an agenda? There were all these rumors flying around that good ole Frederick liked stepping out on his wife."

"Circumstantial, at best." I shook my head. "But it feels right. I can look further into it. *You* will take no more part in this investigation you have started. And you'll come clean about the Instagram page."

Her face crumpled at that. "They'll hate me."

I sighed. She didn't have to say who 'they' were. Her parents. The town. Aleigha was beloved and Margery's actions had put her in direct harm. There was no way around the repercussions that would result from her honesty.

I chewed on my lip, hating that I was rethinking my strategy. "Okay, okay. Let me see what I can do about bringing attention to the case without your name being attached. But I need to be straight with you. There might come a time when you need to step forward."

Margery nodded solemnly, tears still glistening in her eyes. The poor girl was tormented by her mistakes and terrified of what they would mean for her. "I need to get out of this town."

You and me, both. "Let me talk to a friend and see what we can find out, okay? Stay here, stay safe. Call your parents home if you need to. I don't want you disappearing too." I grabbed the folders she had given me. "I'll hold onto these for the time being."

She didn't respond but she swallowed, suddenly fully aware of the potential danger. How it hadn't struck her until now was beyond me but teenagers rarely consider the cost of their actions. I could relate.

I left her tearful and miserable in her bedroom as I exited the house and got into my car. I sat there for a moment, gripping the steering wheel. I hadn't wanted to say anything in the house but if a killer had set their sights on Aleigha, the outlook was grim. My hands tightened on the wheel until my knuckles went white. This might have just gone from a rescue mission to a mission to recover a body. I sighed. Things had gotten complicated.

As I drove back to the library, I kept an eye out for anyone who might be following me. I was suddenly aware that I had not been paranoid the night before. Someone had most likely been following me, wanting to know what I had learned. Did that mean they knew that Aleigha wasn't the one searching for them?

I shot off a text to Margery's parents, instructing them to return home for the safety of their daughter. I received several questioning texts in response but ignored them. The important thing was that they were there. Margery could open up when she felt like she was able to.

I did, however, send a text to Wren letting him know I was on my way with significant evidence. What the evidence meant would be up to us to determine, but suddenly, Mayor Westenberg was looking like a prime candidate for both the 2003 murder *and* the disappearance of Aleigha Morgenstern. Putting my car into gear, I backed out and headed in the direction of my de facto HQ.

Main Street appeared before me quicker than I expected. It was like my body had switched to autopilot the moment I'd pulled out of the Morgenstern's driveway. As the library came into focus, I pulled over and began the trek to the old-fashioned building. As soon as I walked through the doors, I heard a crash.

"Sorry! Sorry! You just, uh, had me a little jumpy," Wren looked over at me sheepishly from an overturned book return cart. He got to his hands and knees and began gathering the scattered volumes.

I strode over quickly and helped him with his task, depositing the books onto the return cart in silence for a moment. It was a weird stalemate. Wren both wanted to know and didn't. I felt uncomfortable beginning the conversation. Finally, Wren broke the heavy silence. "You said you had evidence of some kind. May I ask about which case?"

I sighed and put the last of the books on the return cart carelessly, half of them upside down. "Unfortunately, both. As it turns out, the two cases are almost definitely connected."

I gave him a rundown of my conversation with Margery. As I spoke, I saw him go through a cycle of varying emotions: fear, sadness, confusion. I couldn't blame him. I had come into this town for a simple vacation and ended up uncovering some of this town's darkest crimes. My presence here would change the lives of the townspeople indefinitely. Or maybe it would have happened anyway. Perhaps the police eventually would have made the connection. Still, the weight of where my investigation had led would haunt me.

When I finished, Wren just stood there, undoubtedly wanting to put thought into what he said next. "So, Margery was investigating the two thousand and three cold cases. And she believes... the mayor did it." He sounded skeptical or at least wanting to be.

"I know it sounds a little out there, but I have to say, the evidence—though circumstantial—is pretty damning. I can't say for sure that he's our guy but we might be able to find out with some digging of our own."

Wren blinked, then swallowed. Finally, he turned and walked slowly over the circulation desk, lowering himself into the seat. "Maya, I don't know. If this is in fact, real, the last person who went poking around put someone in the murderer's sights."

I sighed deeply and sank to the floor across from him. I drew my legs up to my chest and rested my arms on my knees. "Yeah. Look, I know the risk. I've run a risk like this before. You, however, have always been a civilian."

Wren remained silent. There was a pained expression on his face that made me silently curse myself for getting him involved in the first place. This hadn't had to be a two person job. I had put another person in jeopardy, unknowingly.

"You can walk away from this," I finished. "I won't judge you in any way. In fact, I shouldn't have come he—"

"No," he said softly. Then again, louder. "No. I want to help. What can I do?"

I pulled the fat folders from my bag and slapped them on the counter, curling my lip. "We have a good amount of this cold case file to look through. Two sets of eyes are better—and faster—than one."

··········

I forgot how dry police documents can be. There was paperwork for every item, every move, every theory, and every suspect (though suspects were few and halfheartedly pursued). Wren and I flipped through them silently, each trying to glean something of importance from their pages.

The rustling of paper was all that could be heard, except when an occasional patron would come in and Wren and I scrambled to tuck away the documents. Each time we pulled them back out, we returned to the evidence with new hope. Hope that something would reveal itself. With another page scanned, I slapped the folder down and looked across the desk at Wren. "Got anything?"

"I mean, I've got a lot. But it's all meaningless. For instance, they found a hair wrapped up in the towel the young woman was found in. It's documented. But paperwork must have gotten lost somewhere. There's no sign of a DNA test run on it. The box was never checked."

I could feel excitement buzzing through me. "Who wrote that report?"

"Um," Wren flipped back a page. "I'll be damned. Frederick Westenberg."

"Clerical error or deliberate coverup?" I had to ask.

"This is still circumstantial, though," he gestured toward the files. "We're just connecting dots without any physical proof."

"The hair."

"You think that hair is still in evidence?" Wren looked skeptical.

"Think about it. You said yourself, the whole force phoned this one in. They didn't know how to properly handle a murder case. A clerical error would be easily overlooked. Missing evidence? That might raise some red flags. Plus, he probably felt untouchable from the inside." The more I talked, the faster the words spilled out of me. Suddenly, I was sure. "We have to check."

Wren looked affronted at the very idea. "Are you saying that after you scolded a child for breaking into a police station mere hours ago, you want to break into a police station?"

I rolled my eyes and waved it off. "No, of course not. But, if we provide the tip anonymously about the cases being tied together, maybe mention the hair... we could be pointing them in the right direction. All perfectly legal. Well, at least on their end. We've already broken a law or two."

Wren took this as well as possible but a shadow of concern crossed his face. "Right. And I'm guessing you're wanting me to leave this anonymous tip?"

I shrugged helplessly with a slight wince. "I can't risk them recognizing my voice and disregarding me because of the chief's opinion of me."

He sighed but I realized it was in resignation. He was willing to do it. Confident in his response, I forged forward. "So, the working theory is that Frederick Westenberg had an affair with Emmaline Rawley. Maybe she was threatening to go to his wife. Maybe she was getting careless. So he murders her to keep their entanglement quiet." I clicked my nails on the desk. "It's plausible. And he'd be in the best position to make sure that no one ever found out about his indiscretions—or murder."

"So, what's our next move?"

"We very well might have physical evidence to tie Westenberg to the crime; however, motive is also important. We can't rely on conjecture. I need to do some digging and see if I can find a connection between the two."

"You're welcome to continue looking through the microfiche of old newspaper articles. In a town like this, all you need to do to find a connection is look there. We sort of announce everything. If they worked on the same volunteer project, we'll know."

"I'll start with the month preceding her death and work from there. It might take a sharp eye but years of scanning legal documents has given me a good eye for that type of thing."

Wren nodded, already heading toward the microfiche room. "Sure thing. I can go ahead and get the right issues for you and leave you to it. I have some restocking to do but give me a shout if you find anything." He paused. "Don't actually shout in the library. Come get me."

·····•·····

As I scanned through yet another issue of the *Landsfield Ridge Gazette*, I grew frustrated. Bake sales, auctions, and community events—but no publicized connection between our victim and the would-be murderer.

I went to flip to the next page of the May 2003 issue before my eyes stopped on a Letter to the Editor piece. The name—Emmaline Rawley. Just 18 at the time—a brand new graduated senior—Emmaline had been granted a ride along for a day to see behind the scenes of the department's day to day. Her letter to the editor was a glowing piece on the way the police were able to keep their small town safe and protected.

It read like propaganda and gave me a bad taste in my mouth. There was no mention of whose cruiser she had been in, but I could take a guess. There was probably a record of it somewhere. And that was just what I needed. A connection. A motive.

Still, there was a question I didn't have an answer to yet. A question that plagued me.

What happened to Aleigha?

Chapter 10

I was still buzzing with excitement as I drove back to my Airbnb that evening. Once I'd found the possible connection, it would take more time to solidify the evidence but it seemed like we had him. We just needed to play it smart from here. Aleigha's disappearance signified that the mayor would do anything to keep his skeletons in the closet. I shuddered to think of what exactly he had done.

The night sky had rapidly swallowed up the brightness of the day, a hallmark of the season. I shivered as I pulled onto the street of the little parsonage, remembering the mark on my door; the car that may or may not have followed me.

I had been onto something. Now, I truly had a solid angle. The case was coming to a close but making the case wouldn't be easy. Pulling into the driveway and turning off the ignition, I clutched my keys for a second. I was close. All I had to do was wait for Wren to call in that anonymous tip and hope the department would listen when I brought the evidence about the connection. The two pieces of evidence together would be damning.

I reached into my bag and pulled out my phone. I suddenly felt the darkness of the town pressing in on me and wanted to hear a comforting voice. I considered calling my mother for just a moment but I didn't want to worry her. I didn't have many friends: One of the downfalls of living for the job.

Before I thought about it too long, I punched in Wren's number and climbed out of the car. As the line rang, I made my way to the front door. I would feel a lot better when I was on the other side of that door, relaxing in a hot bath with a glass of a good merlot. The call connected and Wren came on the line right as I was putting my keys in the door.

"Hey, Maya. You okay?"

"Yeah, I just—" I dropped the phone to my side.

I noticed a flicker of movement in my peripheral vision. I whirled to face the mysterious interloper only to have a cloth pressed over my face. It smelled sterile and sweet. *Chloroform?* Right before everything went black, I was able to slide my phone into the back pocket of my jeans with one hand while halfheartedly slapping at my attacker with the other.

It was fruitless. I knew it. I was caught. Was I about to find out exactly what had happened to Aleigha Morgenstern firsthand?

·····•··•····

When I awoke, I was somewhere dark and damp. The smell was earthy and I could see very little with just the glow of a single lantern in the corner of what I assumed must be a cellar. My head was pounding, surely an after effect of the chloroform. I took in what I could in the dim light. No one was in the cellar with me, friend or foe. So, if Aleigha was still alive, this wasn't where she was being held. I prepared myself for the fact that she wasn't being held anywhere. And that I might share her fate if I didn't do something soon.

I moved from where I was lying and realized that my hands were zip tied behind me. Rookie move. Even for the average civilian, this wasn't a tough spot to get out of. And I was highly trained. Slowly, I shuffled my legs in front of me and looped my arms underneath them so the zip ties were in front. I twisted my wrists slightly, making sure they were crossed and tight before bringing them down hard on my knees, snapping the connection.

Okay, now to make a move. I wandered toward the cellar door only to find that it was locked from the outside. *Of course.* I had, after all, been kidnapped. I was closing in. Suddenly I heard footfalls above me and immediately sprang into action. Or rather, inaction. Not wanting to tip my hand so early, I returned to the spot where I had awoken, placing my hands behind my back as though the zip ties were still there.

There were no obvious weapons in the place so an ambush would probably not work out well for me. However, playing helpless could give me the element of surprise if I was given the right opportunity. The door to the cellar swung open and heavy footfalls descended the stairs. I held my breath, waiting for my captor to show their face.

Fred Westenberg appeared in the dim light of the lantern. His expression was not one I expected. There was no rage there, just grim determination. There was almost a sadness to his eyes as he looked at me. Still, there was also a glint that told me he meant to do me harm.

I shuffled in my position, narrowing my eyes at the mayor. "You."

He sighed, fiddling with something in his right hand. I couldn't make it out in the poor lighting but I made sure to keep an eye on that hand. "Me. Maya, I really thought you'd take my warning more seriously. There was no reason for any more people to get hurt."

The paint on my door. It was Mayor Westenberg.

"You murdered Emmaline Rawley all those years ago to cover up your affair and then you got rid of Aleigha because she was getting too close to the truth."

Fred suddenly looked very tired. "I wish it were that simple."

This surprised me. The evidence was right there and he had taken me. So what part had I gotten wrong? "I wouldn't call that simple. But do tell. What am I missing?"

Fred leaned up against the wall of the cellar and looked down at the earthen ground. "It's true. I was having an affair with Emmaline. She was a precocious, beautiful thing. I couldn't help myself. But I loved her. I did. I know it sounds terrible but it wasn't me who put her in that shallow grave."

My head was spinning with this new information. He had me at his mercy. If he had it his way, I wasn't making it out of this cellar alive. So why deny the murder? Unless...

"Your wife, Sophia. She discovered the affair."

Fred gave a heavy shuddering sigh, and for a moment I almost thought I saw a sheen of tears glisten in his eyes. "I didn't know she knew, at first. But when I found evidence at the crime scene that pointed toward Sophia, I couldn't—" He stopped, the words choking off.

"You didn't want to see her go to prison, so you covered up her crime. Botched the investigation. And it worked, for decades."

The sadness suddenly turned to an icy anger. "And the past should have stayed dead. Sophia has been gone for five years now. What would be the good of bringing this up now, sullying her memory?"

Not to mention your reputation, I wanted to add. But I figured I'd let him keep talking. The longer he talked, the more time I had to find a way to escape or wait for the cavalry I hoped was coming. Surely, Wren had noticed something was wrong when our call dropped so suddenly.

He paced a little and I squirmed where I sat, trying to determine if there was a vantage point I could take advantage of. But attempting to overpower him at this distance would be risky, especially considering that I still couldn't see what was in his hand.

He was still holding it, but the light from the lantern didn't quite reach. It was small, but he held onto it with desperation. *A weapon of some kind?* I couldn't be sure and you never rush a situation before determining all the factors in play.

"It was a shame what I had to do to poor Aleigha, but you have to understand. I was protecting the memory of my wife. She was a good woman. She just—she made a mistake. She was angry. The whole thing was an accident. And this—this girl was going to make her out to be a villain."

I remained stone faced. "You murdered an innocent girl."

"Innocent? She was poking around where she didn't belong. She was *blackmailing* me."

Admittedly, this was news to me. Margery hadn't mentioned a blackmail plot.

"Apparently, my dear wife could not live with what she had done. So she left behind a letter admitting to everything. Somehow, that—that *girl* got ahold of it. I received an anonymous email demanding that I award that sister of hers with the Westenberg Scholarship or the letter would go public."

"And you couldn't let yourself be had," I said with a wry chuckle.

His face contorted in rage. "I couldn't let that little bitch sully my wife's memory. I couldn't let that letter ever get out. So I hired an IT guy to track down the message. It came from a library computer and when I arrived, it was logged into that stupid little Instagram page. So confident and yet so very stupid."

I shook my head. "You have no idea, do you? Aleigha wasn't the one on your trail. That profile poking around asking questions? It was a catfish. She knew nothing. She was innocent."

I watched as the mayor went through shifting emotions. He finally settled on anger. "You're lying. I did what I had to do."

"Believe what you want if you want to remain the hero in your narrative," I said, egging him on. I needed him a bit closer.

He pushed off the wall in a fury. "Honestly, I was somewhat sorry that you would be awake for this, but now..."

I finally got a good look at what he was clutching in his right hand. *A syringe*. Though I couldn't tell on sight what it contained, I knew it was most likely something lethal. Probably how Aleigha met her end. My breath hitched but I calmed my nerves, determined to take control of the situation.

As Frederick moved closer to me, I shifted slightly, making sure my leg was in the correct place for the maneuver I was about to attempt. My life literally depended on executing my infantry training well.

"It'll be over soon, at least," he murmured. Under the anger, there was still that hint of sadness in his words.

As he leaned over me, I swept my leg, knocking him off balance. The syringe dropped from his hand and he glanced over at it for just a moment. But it was a moment I needed. I jumped to my feet in one swift movement and rammed my shoulder into his groin. It was a dirty move but it had a high probability of disarming him long enough. I only needed to buy enough time to run.

Apparently, the mayor was made of tougher stuff. He winced and stumbled for a moment but then came back at me. No longer armed with his syringe, he took a swing with his massive fist. It connected with my chin and tears stung my eyes. I couldn't let the blow stop me, though. Powering through with the sheer force of the will to live, I made a primal sound and tackled Frederick to the ground, grappling him.

We struggled for several moments. He had sheer mass on his side but I had military training. I was fast and efficient. Still, I needed to incapacitate him in order to buy the time to get out of there. I aimed a blow at his head with my elbow.

Pain shot up my arm and a welt began to appear on Frederick's head but he remained conscious. He was dazed though, his eyes getting cloudy with disorientation. I had him pinned but he was still struggling and his weight was bucking against me, attempting to toss me off. I almost missed his hand reaching for the fallen syringe.

As his hands closed around it, he attempted to jab me with the needle, ending the struggle then and there. But I was able to pin his arm in a position that made it impossible. With a grunt of exertion, I gritted my teeth and leaned my knee into his already injured groin area. He shouted out in anger and pain, grabbing at my arms. He was attempting to overpower me and I was still somewhat dazed by the chloroform. It was looking like it would be a test of endurance.

Suddenly, he gained the upper hand, shifting his weight and managing to knock me off balance. Our positions had switched and he was on top, the syringe hovering inches above my face. I was prepared to fight with everything I had left but suddenly, the outlook was looking grim.

"Maya! Maya are you here?"

The voice came from above. It was the chief. I almost sighed in relief before managing to gasp, "Down here! Quickly!"

There were sounds of several heavy footfalls above me. The cellar door swung open and police officers poured in. They took in the scene, puzzled. Whatever they'd been told about the situation, they had not expected to see us grappling for the upper hand.

"Help me," I said, somewhat breathless.

The stunned officers immediately sprang into action, dragging the mayor off of me, knocking the deadly syringe from his hands. I finally felt like I could breathe easier as more police officers poured in, guns drawn.

Thank you, Wren. I massaged my sore wrists as one of the officers put Frederick Westenberg in handcuffs. As they read him his rights and led him out, I let myself have a moment of satisfaction. I hadn't been able to save Aleigha as I had hoped but I had given her justice.

The chief walked up to me, a grim expression on his face. "Didn't I tell you to stay out of this?"

I managed a wobbly grin of sheepishness. "Not really my style. Sorry."

He sighed and shook his head but I thought I saw a hint of humor in his expression. "Well, it looks like you kept digging and really found something." He scratched his head and watched as the uniformed officers took the mayor up the cellar stairs. "Frederick Westenberg—I never would have guessed. He always seemed like such a stand-up guy."

I joined him in watching the procession, grimly. "It was all about secrets and lies, trying to keep them covered up. I think even the most clean-cut person you can find has a skeleton or two hiding in their closet."

The chief blew out a deep breath. "Usually not ones this dark."

"You'd be surprised."

"So, how did you land on Frederick Westenberg, anyway? I got an anonymous tip that sounded a lot like that librarian you've been buddy-buddy with. And then I get a call that you're in danger and here we are."

I coughed, suddenly feeling drained and disoriented now that the adrenaline had worn off. "I can give you the highlights. But first, can we get the hell out of here?"

Chapter 11

Frederick agreed to lead the authorities to Aleigha's body, probably in exchange for some kind of leniency. She had been much more carefully disposed of than Emmaline Rawley, giving credence to his version of the 2003 events. Aleigha had been buried deep within the woods behind the old school building that had been shut down in the 50s, her remains covered in lyme. I was long gone by the time the body was discovered but my stomach turned at the very thought. A life so tragically cut short by secrets and lies. Left to rot at the age of 16 in an unmarked grave.

The family—and the entire town—was devastated. I watched from my hospital bed as careless vultures attempted to shove cameras in the faces of the grieving parents, catching them outside the police department, asking them about the deal Frederick Westenberg had cut with the DA. Their tear streaked faces said it all—lives shattered. The cold reality of a life without their youngest daughter.

It wasn't the local news I was watching. The case had—unsurprisingly—made statewide headlines and even some national ones. It seemed the cynical passing of time loved to see the image of the idyllic small town crumbling under the weight of its own secrets.

Of course, that meant my involvement had been made known. The call from my mother had not been a particularly gentle one. She damn near lost it when I told her I was currently in the hospital due to my involvement. Even though I specified it was strictly for observation due to a mild concussion. In the end, she told me she was proud and to come visit sometime. Moms, they still love their children, no matter how reckless they are.

She hadn't been the only caller. Colleagues had called to check in on me, having seen my name on national news. And a few visitors trickled in. Wren came by with a balloon bouquet and a dorky grin with a promise he'd return every day to keep me company (which he had). Lili stopped in to check on me too, but really seemed to just want some good gossip. And the Morgenstern's had made a brief, heartbreaking visit during which they thanked me through gut-wrenching tears.

I grinned and bore it. It was all I could do. I knew the news was heralding me as a hero. But was I, really? Aleigha was not home safe. She was gone. I hadn't saved anyone. I had just peeled back the layers of the town until I'd found the seedy underbelly.

Landsfield Ridge would never be the same. Emmaline Rawley's memory haunted the town. They spoke her name in whispers but never wanted to speak of her lingering ghost. Until a clueless stranger had strolled into town and imploded their lives.

Of course—I tried to reason—the truth mattered. After all, if I hadn't revealed the truth of the Rawley murder, then the truth of Aleigha's disappearance might not have come out. It would have been another injustice—another haunting in the town. I wondered how much that mattered right now to the people in Landsfield Ridge.

"Knock, knock."

I looked up to see Wren carrying takeout containers. I couldn't help it. It brought a warm smile to my face. "Hey, Wren."

"So, I was thinking to myself—you know what sucks about hospital stays?"

"Everything?"

He shook his head, taking on a look of mock seriousness. "No, the food! The food here is unseasoned cardboard. I had an appendectomy a few years back and man, I dreamed of some good Thai food." He plopped the takeout containers down on the table beside the hospital bed and seated himself in the chair opposite me.

"You have a point," I said, eyeing the pad thai with a grumbling stomach. "I think the mashed potatoes last night were mostly water."

He laughed easily, as he began laying out the spread on my tray table. He was smiling but there was a weariness to him. A weariness I'd seen in everyone who had walked through that door. His town was imploding but he was here with supplies. I watched him as he worked, playing tetris with the food containers on the small surface.

He was something special and he didn't even see it. He was a glimmer of kindness and hospitality in a world where most were just looking to keep their own secrets. He had—apparently—even accompanied the officers to the cellar once he told them of his suspicions. He had been in the cellar once, during a charity event. He knew where it was and figured he could guide them there faster on his own.

And yet, he still had no idea how remarkable he was. I hoped this town never stole his spark because it was well earned. I started thinking about my rules and ideas about dating as I watched him. Of course, he wasn't a viable candidate, no matter how marvelous he'd been in action. But maybe entanglements weren't the distraction I believed them to be.

"So, your, uh, vacation is over soon?" Wren said, as he handed me a plastic fork and pushed the pad thai forward.

I rolled my eyes as I stabbed my fork into the steaming noodles. "Ah yes, my relaxing vacation is coming to a close. I'm sure this town will be glad to see me go."

"I mean, not all of it."

"Wren..."

"I don't just mean me. There are plenty of people in this town who are really grateful. There was a murderer in our midst. A child murderer at that and you got him out of our lives. That's something we are incredibly grateful for. Maybe once the dust settles, the rest will come around. It's just... a lot."

There was sincerity there. An earnest belief. But I wasn't sure if I was convinced. Darkness had seeped out of the shadows in Landsfield Ridge and taken center stage. It would take longer than Wren wanted to believe for "the dust to settle."

"I'll miss you, ya know." I said it without thinking.

Wren looked up from his curry in surprise. "Oh, really? Yes, I was wondering what you would do without your Scooby gang member."

I laughed softly. "I'll manage, I'm sure. But it *will* be tough."

"I'll miss you too," he said with complete sincerity. "I never trusted ole Fred anyway. And... you made me feel like I was part of something for the first time in a long time. I just—I wanted to thank you for that gift."

"You shouldn't view it as a gift. View it as what you deserve, Wren. Because you do." I waved my arms. "But enough about the case. I feel like I'm a bit overloaded on all of that now."

Wren smiled and for the first time, I noticed a slight dimple in his left cheek. "Alright. So tell me, why an attorney?"

I hadn't been expecting that. "What do you mean?"

He shrugged and smashed the rice in his curry with the back of his spoon. "I mean, you might be good in a courtroom. But out in the field like that? Why not stick with the armed forces, join the military police?"

I thought about it for a moment. "It started out as something for my dad. But I realized too late that what he had given me was a gift. He helped me find the best way to channel my desire for justice."

"That sounds like a hell of a gift."

I was trying to consider what to say next when I heard someone softly tap on the door to my hospital room. The knock sounded timid, unsure. Margery Morgenstern was standing in the doorway, looking pale and miserable. Her eyes were bloodshot and watery, whether from crying or lack of sleep, I didn't know. She took in the scene between Wren and me and her mouth made a little 'o.' She began to back out of the room.

"Sorry, I can come back later. I didn't realize you have company already."

Wren and I shared a brief, meaningful look. It was strange that we were somehow so on the same wavelength after such a short time as partners. But he understood exactly what my glance meant and quickly stood up.

"Actually, you're just in time. I forgot about dessert and was just about to head out and grab some over at Jenny's."

Margery looked unsure but remained where she stood, looking between the two of us. Finally, she forced a small smile on her face. "Then I'll keep her company while you make the ice cream run."

He nodded, as if in thanks to Margery, and left the hospital room quietly. He let the door slide shut on his way out, undoubtedly his way of giving me and Margery a bit more privacy for our conversation. We weren't in Landsfield Ridge anymore but Santa Rosa wasn't much bigger by comparison. People talked.

"It's good to see you, Margery," I said gently, not quite sure how to engage this particular conversation I had been dreading for days.

Margery shook her head and looked like she wanted to cry but was too exhausted to manage it. "Don't say that. It's not true. I'm the reason you're here. I'm the reason for all of this."

With a stern look, I leveled my gaze at her. "Frederick Westenberg is the reason for all of this. You made a rookie mistake. You're a kid. He is a grown man who knew what he was doing."

She sank down into the chair Wren had just occupied and stared absently out the window. "The cops know there was a catfish profile digging into the 0' three case. They know it's what caused Aleigha's disappearance. They don't know it's me, yet."

I sighed, trying to keep my tone even. I needed her to hear me. "Margery, I kept your name out of it as long as I could. But Wren and I uncovered your identity in days. The cops have more and better resources at their disposal than a vacationer and a librarian."

Her eyes widened and she swallowed. I didn't need to say the next part, but I did anyway. "You need to let them know it was you before they find out for themselves. It will go better for you if your parents and the police hear it from you first." I looked intently into her eyes. "You are not to blame for this, okay? We've been over that. But the whole story will come out and you'll want to be the one telling your side."

She nodded, but a tiny gasping sob escaped her throat. "She was their everything and I am part of the reason she's gone."

I thought again of the mantle with Aleigha in the spots of honor. I thought of how they had spoken of her. Of how Margery had spoken when I'd cornered her. "Your parents aren't perfect people. And they may have had Aleigha on a pedestal. But you are still their daughter and they love you."

"Not like they loved her," she murmured, almost to herself rather than to me.

I didn't know how to respond. Maya Hartwell, the fast-talking attorney, was at a loss. I couldn't begin to understand their family dynamics and didn't know what I could say to comfort this girl. There was so much complexity and I had tipped a delicate balance when I revealed Margery's secrets.

I gazed at the flowers a well-wisher had sent as I spoke my next words to her, very carefully. "The thing about small towns is that when you grow up in them, they feel like your entire world. Everyone knows everyone and the world seems so small. But when you leave it behind, this whole new world opens up to you and you realize it wasn't as small as you had pictured. And you find a place for yourself somewhere.

"This town was poisoned long before Frederick Westenberg took your sister. It's a town of distrust and archaic social hierarchies. Join a journalism program at a college far away. Get the hell out of dodge. Find a place where you are seen as enough."

The speech wasn't rehearsed but it flowed from my lips like it was a practiced piece. "I had yearned to get away to a small community and found that it had its own problems. The world is a broken place. But you found somewhere you could make a difference and you hunkered down."

Margery looked at me, her eyes swimming with tears. There was grief there but there was also a new resolve. She had heard me. Good. One less soul lost to the toxic cycle of Landsfield Ridge. Without saying another word, she nodded slightly and exited the room.

It was the last time I ever saw her. At least, in person. She appeared on the news several times in the weeks following, her yearbook photo now tied to the coverage of the case that had "rocked small town America." The last I had heard of her, she was planning to attend a small private university off the northeast coast.

I closed my eyes as she closed the door behind her and let myself relax. The hospital linens were scratchy, but I knew that in a day's time I'd be discharged and headed back to my own bed. I smiled at the thought, as I slowly started to melt into sleep.

Chapter 12

I sat in my office chair watching a blinking cursor. It was Monday morning and I was supposed to be in attorney mode. In the week I had been gone, my inbox had filled up and I was hoping to respond to a few emails before my meeting with Alfred Richards but I couldn't seem to put the past week behind me.

I had left a by-the-books attorney, someone who had left her sleuthing days behind her for more practical and legal pursuits. But in the course of one week, I'd thrown myself into my old life. I had liked it, too. It felt perverse—given the fallout of my findings—but I had taken some joy in uncovering the truth. I imagined my father was proud, wherever he was. I'd never been all that religious but I still felt like he looked down on me from time to time. I figured that he had been watching my entire investigation with the eyes of a knowing father.

It felt strange now, returning to this world of affidavits and office memos. Still, it was the other side of me. While investigating was exciting and even necessary, revealing the truth was never enough. There had to be order to law and order.

Frederick Westenberg wouldn't stand trial, if I had heard correctly. He was in talks for a plea deal, as the evidence against him had been overwhelming. However, there were many other cases that depended on a proper trial; the right representation, the right jury. That's where I came in, as often as I could. Though my work in Landsfield Ridge had been important, so too was my work here. I sighed and attempted to shake off the week's events before responding to the next email. My meeting with Alfred Richards was in twenty minutes and I still had work to do.

I still wasn't quite sure what the meeting was about. After the big pharmaceutical case, I was hoping it would mean a promotion; perhaps a nicer office. Something that recognized my hard work. In fact, I was a little eager, keeping one eye on the clock.

When the time finally came, I stood from my chair and locked my computer. I took out the compact mirror from my briefcase to ensure that I looked presentable for a meeting with a senior partner. Content that nothing was askew or out of place, I made my way toward the elevator banks. I punched the button for the elevator and fidgeted with my father's watch as I waited for it to arrive. Though I was a powerhouse in the courtroom, I often found myself growing nervous in office settings. The politics of a law firm could quickly grow complicated and I had my own baggage to deal with in that area.

Finally, as the elevator doors opened with a small ding, I stepped inside and found myself standing next to a well-dressed man in a sharp gray suit. While my outfit couldn't compare to the apparent cost of his watch, I've always believed in dressing my best as it seems to appeal to clients. Of course, the quality of our work should always speak for itself, but many of our clients seem to place value on appearances, and I strive to meet their expectations. I used to question the idea that designer clothing was essential for court appearances, I now appreciate the importance of presenting oneself in the best possible light.

I nodded politely to him as I pushed the button for floor 12—the floor where only partner offices were located. A warmth of pride flooded through my body. It was a rare appointment that took me to this floor, as a mere junior associate.

The elevator doors opened for my fellow passenger on floor 10 and he got off with a small wave. I waved back absently but my mind was already willing the doors to close so I could be on my way. When I arrived on the 12th floor, I took in the opulence of my surroundings. They had spared no expense in decorating this floor. Everything from the wood trim to the carpeting looked luxurious and decadent. I knew that Richards's office was in the corner on the northeast side, so I made my way in that direction.

As I arrived at his secretary's desk, she gave me a pleasant enough smile, though it didn't quite reach her eyes. "Hi, do you have an appointment with Mr. Richards?"

"Yes, a nine-thirty appointment. I think I am a few minutes early."

The secretary typed a few things into her sleek laptop and responded without looking back up at me. "You are, but that's fine. His eight-thirty finished early." Before I could say anything, she hit a button on her phone and spoke into it. "Your nine-thirty has just arrived." There was a pause while she listened to his reply.

Before I had a chance to speak, the door to the office opened and Alfred Richards stood in his doorway, a broad smile on his face. "Hartwell. It's so good to see you again. I heard you had quite a week. Come on in!" He beckoned me into his office.

I entered the office and was surprised to find a contrast between the interior and the reception area. While the reception area was all plush and warm, Richards's office was all metal and polished. Very chic and modern. I felt like I might cut myself by accident just sitting in the severe looking chair across from his desk.

"So," he began, "First of all, I want to say that I'm glad you are doing well after your little excursion up north. I hear you were quite integral in building the case against Frederick Westenberg. That's commendable."

I nodded but I was suddenly getting a sinking feeling in my stomach. I knew how the partners operated. If they started in too early with the compliments, they were setting you up to soften a blow. I shifted uncomfortably in my chair.

"Now, I also wanted to commend you on a job well done on the Alanzi Pharmaceutical case. It was a tough one but you did a remarkable job. We were all quite impressed. Quite impressed."

Yikes, strike two. He was repeating himself. A stall tactic. "Thank you for your kind words. As you know, though, the Alanzi case was a team effort. I couldn't have done it without my colleagues and the hard work of my paralegals." It was a line I was supposed to say in this little dance. I had primarily done the legwork. And he knew it, to be honest.

"Of course. I am glad you agree on that front. Remarkable performance; I believe Blaine Laughlin was of great assistance in building the case, am I correct?"

I gritted my teeth slightly. Blaine Laughlin was another junior partner who had 'assisted' my efforts. Which is to say, he retrieved some documents for me and had since been claiming he was integral to the case's success. It didn't really bother me that much. Most knew the truth. Right?

Richards leaned across his desk, folding his hands in front of him. "Now, I know you were aware of an opening for a senior associate at the firm. Over the course of the last few months, you and Blaine were our front runners. It was close. Very close. But we have decided to go with Blaine on this."

My jaw dropped. Not metaphorically. My mouth literally fell open in sheer shock. It took me a moment to regain my composure. "I realize that Blaine is a valuable colleague but *I* ran lead on that case. I don't understand."

On his part, Richards looked slightly affronted at my perfectly reasonable response. "Well, we looked at much more than one case. We looked at performance over time."

"I still believe that makes me a stronger candidate."

"We also considered seniority and firm image."

That stopped me in my tracks. "Firm... image?"

Richards shook his head and sighed, slapping a newspaper down on his desk. I guess people still read these outside of Landsfield Ridge. "This excursion up north—while impressive—also gives you a bit of a reputation."

"With all due respect, I already had a reputation. I've helped solve more than just this one case."

He sighed again, this time a deep theatrical gust. "That's just the problem, Maya. You see, some clients view you as a loose cannon. They want their matters handled by someone more by-the-book. More," he tried to search for the right word, "level-headed."

I always thought the phrase "you could have knocked me over with a feather" was a hyperbolic cliché but I could feel my legs turn to putty. I swallowed the growing lump in my throat and looked him straight in the eye, seething. They wanted someone a little more male was more like it. What would have been heroic if done by Blaine was seen as flighty because I was a woman. And it had cost me what I had wanted most.

I silently cursed Frederick Westenberg. The press. The whole damn situation. But I didn't let a bit of it show on my face. They wanted level-headed? "I see. Well, I wish Blaine the best of luck. I'm sure he'll be an excellent choice." I began collecting my briefcase. "If that is all, I should get back to work."

"Maya, I understand your disappointment, but know that the race was very close. You will see your day in the sun. I don't want this to discourage you."

"Oh, it hasn't." I moved toward the door and then turned back to face him. "I'm going to make it damn near impossible for you not to promote me next time."

I watched his face and something flicked across it quickly. I think he was somewhat impressed with my response. *Never let them see you sweat, Hartwell. It's the only way to survive in this shark tank.*

I spent the rest of the day "catching up on paperwork" when really, I was distracted by the meeting. It shouldn't have gotten under my skin the way that it had. But after accomplishing what I had in two consecutive weeks, to be overlooked felt like a slap to the face.

At 3:12 p.m., I set an away message to my email status and left the office, headed for home. I put on Pink Floyd again, blasting "Lost for Words" and sang the lyrics poorly, as loudly as I could. Despite having just come off vacation, it was the first time I felt truly relaxed in weeks.

I listened to David Gilmour's words and soaked in the themes, letting the familiar music soothe me. This had always been Dad's favorite album and it had become mine when he introduced it to me. At an appropriate age, of course. "There's an F bomb, for goodness sake," my mother had said.

I listened to the album the rest of the way home, the commute as easy as it was earlier in the afternoon. I took the long way home, looking around at the city that surrounded me. The marvels it held, the secrets it kept. It was similar to Landsfield Ridge in that way.

As I finally arrived home, I dropped my briefcase and keys unceremoniously by the door and headed into the kitchen. I poured myself a tall glass of Bone Ash Vineyard Cabernet, slightly hypnotized as the dark liquid swirled into the glass. It looked too much like blood and my stomach curdled. I decided to pour it down the drain and reached for a Diet Coke instead.

Popping the tab, I wandered into my bedroom, grabbing my eReader. Ignoring the news page, I scrolled to a romance novel and let my mind wander free in a place of fantasy. Where wrongs were righted and there was always a happily ever after.

Real stories often don't end that way and we try to tell ourselves it's okay. But it's the sign of a broken world hurting people. Promotion or not, I had done my best to right the wrongs of a damaged society. I had gotten smacked down, but that was just part of the cycle.

There would always be another wrong to right. Another case to pursue. I was confident that this stumbling block would not be a permanent detour. There would be a happily ever after for me in this world. But, as I had told Margery, I would have to carve my own place in it first. It would take sweat, tears, and hours I would never get back. But I wasn't in the job for the approval, no matter how desperately I wanted it. I was in it because of a beautiful gift from father to daughter—a legacy handed down.

Realizing I hadn't been absorbing any of the book I'd been reading, I tapped back to the news page and found another headline of misjustice. A police brutality case from the looks of it. Sighing, I jotted the details down, wondering if I could act as legal counsel as my pro bono job for the year.

There really was no rest for the wicked.

Heads Up! – Here is the back cover blurb to **Room of Echoes (Quest for Justice) Series Book 2** in the series, released **May 2023**

Embark on an enticing journey alongside a renowned civil lawyer as she transitions from handling cases centered around financial compensation to tackling the intense realm of military murder defense.

Get ready to dive into the thrilling world of Maya Hartwell, a young and headstrong attorney who takes her responsibilities seriously. With a growing number of successful cases under her belt, Maya is on the path to a promising career. But her life takes a dramatic turn when she receives a phone call from her dear friend Isabella, falsely accused of murder in war-torn Afghanistan.

Maya is determined to save her friend, plunging headfirst into her most perplexing and perilous case yet. As she investigates, Maya finds herself unexpectedly caught up in the shadows of her family's past, including her father's death, which she discovers was not an accident.

With no turning back, Maya must navigate a network of falsehoods and deceit to uncover the truth in a Room of Echoes. Will she be able to win in this ultimate fight for life and justice? Don't miss a moment of this pulse-pounding legal thriller as Maya fights to clear her friend's name and bring the real murderers to justice.

Up Next for Maya Hartwell - Books in the series;

Echoes of the Past (Quest for Justice) Series Book – Published on Amazon. **https://books2read.com/u/baq9O2**

Room of Echoes (Quest for Justice) Series Book 2 – Published on Amazon **https://books2read.com/u/m0WqvA**

Echoes of Betrayal (Quest for Justice) Series Book 3 - Published on Amazon **https://books2read.com/u/mZq97B**

Book 4 in the Quest for Justice Series Coming Q2 2024 or sooner!

Newsletter Sign Up

You can find out more about my books and any up coming news at my website via this link **www.gabbyblack.com** or indeed just sign up for my newsletter by going to the website.

About The Author

Get ready to embark on an exciting journey into the captivating world of mystery, courtroom drama, crime, and investigation with Gabby Black's thrilling novels. As an ardent enthusiast of these genres, I pour my heart and soul into weaving stories that will keep you eagerly turning the pages, filled with suspense, unexpected plot twists, and enigmatic mysteries that will keep you guessing until the very last word.

With a background spanning nine years in the Justice System, I draw upon both my vivid imagination and real-life experiences to craft gripping tales that will leave you absolutely spellbound. When I'm not immersed in writing, I'm out there exploring the world through travel, connecting with diverse people, seeking out new adventures, and drawing inspiration for my next novel. Oh, and did I mention I'm a lover of fine wine, well lets be honest its actually most wine! You might have picked up on that from the pages of my books.

So, won't you join me on this exhilarating journey into the unknown, where every page holds the promise of discovery and excitement? Grab one of my novels and let's dive into a world where thrilling stories await, and unforgettable adventures are just a page turn away. Cheers to the mysteries that lie ahead!

Thank you so much for reading and I sincerely hope you enjoyed the third book in the new 'Quest for Justice' series. As an independent author, I am incredibly grateful for your support. I would love if you could take just a few moments to write a review. Your reviews are immensely helpful and I do genuinely read each and every single one. For those of you who are reading from an ipad, phone or pc here is a direct link to leave a review **https://rebrand.ly/1d6iumz** otherwise kindly log into your Amazon account, find the book and leave a review. I truly appreciate your time and feedback. Thanks Immensely!

You can find out more about me and my books at at my website via this link **www.gabbyblack.com**

Printed in Great Britain
by Amazon

42182653R00078